KISS ME HARD

KISS ME HARD

THOMAS B. DEWEY

(writing as Tom Brandt)

WILDSIDE PRESS

Copyright © 1953 by Thomas B. Dewey.

Published by Wildside Press LLC.
www.wildsidebooks.com

CHAPTER 1

You know these Midwest towns: the long, wide main street—eight or ten blocks of stores—with the railroad cutting across it at one end and maybe a park with a bandstand at the other; with tree-lined streets stretching away on both sides, past high, old-fashioned frame houses; and all around, the flat, green-brown farmlands: and somewhere, between a couple of stores, a tavern, serving light wines and beer and maybe hard liquor too, depending on the local customs and the latest election.

A tavern like this might have, for entertainment, a television set, a jukebox and a handful of local wits. Hardly ever would it have a live musician, a piano player. A really good, self-respecting piano player has it tough enough in a city, with a saloon in every block. And a guy running a small-town spot doesn't make enough to pay half the union scale for a keyboard hack who can play "Beautiful Ohio" so it sounds like "Hearts and Flowers" and accompany the local quartet in "Tie Me to Your Apron Strings Again." So you don't find piano players in the small-town taverns.

But at one time, this particular tavern in this particular town in "Beautiful Ohio" did have a piano player and I was it. I'd been there a week. I'd done pretty well the first week—eight bucks in the kitty and the boss never let my beer glass get empty. I carried a small bottle of my own besides and with the beer, I got along all right, which is to say I would be in a deep, comfortable fog by one A.M., my normal condition.

The work was easy. The customers weren't hard to please. I gave them straight stuff, cut very square, without riffs, runs or razzle-dazzle. Sometimes I felt guilty. But most of the time I just kept the beer going down and relaxed. It might have gone on for a long time, if it hadn't been for this redhead...

She'd been in the joint every night for a week—a girl with red hair, a bold-faced girl with a ripe bosom pushing through the summer dress, with fine legs and well-turned ankles and her hips pleasantly rounded on the bar stool. I'd noticed her, the way you notice certain girls, but I'd only taken a look now and then and minded my own business. She was a local girl and I was a stranger, playing the piano in a tank-town tavern.

Sometimes she would be alone, stay for an hour or two, drinking beer, listening to the music, and sometimes she would be with a guy. It was always the same guy, a big bruiser with a thick neck, and hands like a gorilla's, with stiff, black hair all over the backs of them. He never paid any attention to the piano and he didn't pay much attention to the girl. You could see they were together and that he was the guy in her life, but they didn't have much to say to each other. He had a few cronies he hung around with and sometimes he wouldn't speak to the girl until it was time to go home. Even then it might be only a nod or a shake of the head.

So I didn't stick my nose in. I had this good thing and I wanted to keep it. Once in a while I would glance up and the girl would be staring at me, listening to the music. I would throw her a professional smile and then get my eyes back on the keyboard—not that I had to look at it, but I felt safer that way.

Then, this particular night, the girl decided she didn't want it like that. She had come in early and sat at the bar for a while. Later she moved to a table twelve inches from the treble end of the keyboard. It was too early for a crowd and besides the bartender and me there were only the redhead and one skinny, bookkeeperish type character, who sat at the far end of the bar, nursing a short beer.

The girl sat alone at the table, drinking beer, and the scent of her perfume came over strong and sharp. I'd slept most of the day and hadn't had a chance to drink much yet, so I was a little edgy. I kept my eyes off her. It was bad public relations, but it was easier on my nerves. After a while she leaned forward and asked for a match, though there was a packet stuck in the ash tray on her table. When I reached across to hold the light for her, she held my hand steady with both of hers and as she dragged in on the cigarette her eyes went over my face slowly.

"How do you like our town?" she asked through a smoke ring.

"O.K.," I said and went back to the job.

She raised her voice.

"What's your name?"

"Chris," I said. "Chris Cross."

She laughed. Naturally. Funny thing is, that's my name. Christopher Cross. My old man had a hell of a sense of humor.

The redhead leaned forward.

"You don't look like a piano player," she said. "You look more like a stevedore."

"That's what they told me at the conservatory."

The bartender came over to replace an empty glass and he left two instead of one. When I lifted my eyebrows, he nodded toward the girl. I raised my glass in thanks and she smiled and moved onto the bench with me. It was a small bench and her left thigh pressed hard against my right one.

"You want to play too?" I asked.

"Not on the piano."

Right along in there I began to get scared. In spite of the legends and all the books about it, there aren't many women who go after you like that, straight and direct, and when it happens, if you're leery of women anyway, it scares you off.

The bartender went to the back room and the girl pressed closer and spoke into my ear.

"My name's Hazel," she said.

Since she was a customer and a native, I couldn't very well spit in her face. I had to brush her off, but cool and slow, so it wouldn't make trouble.

"I'm a little shy," I said. "Also, I have to work."

"You'll get off sometime, won't you?"

"Sure. Midnight."

When the bartender came back, she got off the piano bench and went back to her table. Some more customers came in and after a while she got up to leave. The big guy with the hairy hands hadn't shown up. On her way out, she paused long enough to stick something in the kitty—a beer glass on top of the old upright. What she put in was a couple of bills wrapped around a piece of white paper. She flashed a deadpan at me and went out.

Between numbers I snaked the piece of paper out of the kitty and looked at it. She'd written:

"615 East Chestnut Street. Hazel."

I put it in my pocket, took a short break and went back to the piano. It was a slow night and I fooled around for a while with some arrangements I'd been working on for a dozen years. But they didn't go so well. I had stopped being serious about music a long time ago and a lot of it I had forgotten. What I tried only sounded sloppy, and nobody in the joint cared anyway. I went into the straight, easy stuff and tried to relax.

I couldn't get Hazel off my mind. I couldn't forget the rich, red hair, the breasts pushing through the summer dress, the generous hips, the good legs. I couldn't forget the scent of her when she leaned close to me on the piano bench. I said I'm leery of women. But I'm not made of wood. I'm not immune.

Take it easy, I kept telling myself. She's a local girl. She's married. Let her play with somebody else.

By the time we closed for the night I had pretty well talked myself out of it. I hung around for a while and helped the bartender put the tavern in order for the next day. Then he locked up and I walked up the street a couple of blocks to the run-down hotel I was living in.

It was after one o'clock and the town had folded up for the night. The stores and houses were dark and there was nobody on the streets. The hotel was a four-story brick building on a corner. There were two entrances, one on the main street and another around the corner on the side street, the one I used because it depressed me to go through the lobby, past the ancient, feeble night clerk who always went to sleep standing up.

When I rounded the corner I saw a cream-colored Ford convertible parked at the curb opposite the small side entrance with the yellow light bulb over the door. I didn't pay much attention at first, because the car lights were out and I couldn't see that there was anybody sitting in it. I headed for the door and had turned into it when the car lights blinked a couple of times. I glanced around and saw somebody behind the wheel. The lights blinked again and I walked slowly to the car.

I guess I really knew all the time who it would be.

The top of the convertible was down and I leaned on the door and looked across the seat at her.

"Surprise," she whispered.

"Yeah," I said. "I got your invitation, but I couldn't make it."

Earlier, in the tavern, she had worn her hair up, very fancy and neat, with a high pile of it across the top. But now she had let it down and it was spread out around her face and over the back of the seat behind her head. The scent of her perfume was stronger than ever.

I was carrying a perfect load. I felt sure of myself and untouchable. At this point, I would be hard to scare. It was not the same now as it had been in the joint when she'd sat beside me at the keyboard.

Her eyes were looking at me through the dark, out of her beautiful pink and white face.

"Is there something about me you don't like?" she said softly.

"Two things," I said.

I could see her jump slightly.

"What?" she said.

"The ring you're wearing," I said, "and that big bastard I've seen you with."

She looked away from me. Her left arm was resting on the wheel and her fingers played with the spokes in it. Her perfume was filling the whole street—or maybe it was just filling me.

"That 'big bastard,'" she said, "is my husband. Let's say—he doesn't understand me."

"And you, what do you understand?"

"Let's say I'm a music lover."

I looked up and down the street.

"Isn't it risky for you to sit here talking to me, this time of the night?" I said. "In a little town like this?"

She shrugged.

"It would be safer if you'd get in and we'd go for a ride," she said.

I figured I'd done my duty. I'd played hard to get as long as any man could be expected to. I twisted the handle of the door, opened it and slid in beside her. She straightened behind the wheel.

"You want to drive?" she said.

"Better not," I said. "I'm loaded."

She looked at me quickly.

"How loaded?"

"Just enough," I said, "which is too much to drive."

I knew I would need another drink before long, but I had some left in the bottle in my pocket. It wouldn't be safe for me to drive, but I was all right for everything else, for a couple of hours anyway.

She got the car started and pulled away from the curb, heading for the main street. She turned left into it and drove slowly toward the north end of town. We crossed a bridge over a small creek and then we were in the country, with flat fields and occasional farm buildings on both sides of the road. She drove faster now and in the rushing night air the odor of her perfume was mingled with the smell of clover and alfalfa in the fields along the road.

You can't talk much in an open convertible and I didn't have much to say anyway. It was her party. So I leaned back in the seat and let the wind beat me in the face and watched her thick, red hair blowing as we rode.

After about ten minutes she slowed suddenly and turned off the road into a narrow lane that wound upward among trees. The trees grew so close to the road they brushed the car as we passed. The air smelled damp, as if we were near a river or as if the ground were wet. The ruts of the lane were deep and I held onto the door handle as we lurched up the low hill.

The car bumped heavily as Hazel turned into a clearing, drifted to a stop and turned off the lights. There was a bright moon and looking across the seat, I could see her clearly—her beautiful face, surrounded by that hair and the rich, ripe swelling of her breasts. She was truly a gorgeous pile of woman.

We sat there for a while, neither of us speaking. The night was quiet. The white moonlight filled the small clearing. I took a deep breath and sprawled in the seat.

"Los Angeles was never like this," I said.

"That's where you're from?" Hazel asked.

"Some time back."

"What made you stop in a hick town like this?"

"I got hungry," I said. "Even a lush gets hungry once in a while. Also thirsty."

Hazel's fingers were worrying at the steering wheel again. Her eyes stared off somewhere. After a while she clenched her right fist and began to pound it on the wheel, steadily in a light, thudding pattern.

"At least you got away," she said.

"No," I said. "You never get away."

"You must have got away from something—or somebody—whatever it was eating on you."

"It was myself eating on me."

I felt her shudder.

"Did we come out here to be philosophers?" I said.

I turned in the seat and looked at her face. She let me grab and hold her eyes. We stared at each other.

"No," she whispered.

Her face moved toward mine. I reached for her and she came against me. Our lips met and hers were quivering. She made a low sound in her throat.

I ran out of breath and pulled away. I drew her across my lap and held her in the crook of my arm. She lay with her head back, her eyes closed, her thick hair tumbled against the door of the car.

"Chris—" she said. "Take me away from here—from this damn town."

"Sure," I mumbled. "Anything you say."

My mouth was on hers, my lips searching. She held my face in her hands, staring at me.

"I mean it, Chris," she said. "I've got to get away. It's been in the cards a long time, but I never had the nerve, not by myself. I need help."

"O.K.," I said, trying to free my face, but she held it more tightly.

"I've got a little money—this car. We could start out and keep going. They'd never find us. If you'll help me get away, Chris, there won't be any strings. You can come and go as you please—" She had lifted her head and her eyes were boring into mine. My brain was foggy and I wanted to get on with what we had started. I kept thinking, what a thing to hold out for. If you want to leave, why don't you take your car and go?

I guess she read my mind.

"I've been alone too long, Chris," she was saying. "I'm afraid of the lonesomeness. If I went away by myself, I'd be more alone than ever. I can't stand that. Not at first. I've got to have somebody help me over the hump."

I tried to pull myself together.

"You know how it feels to be on the run?" I said.

"I don't care. It can't be any worse than this—living with a pig, in a dead, narrow-minded town where nobody ever has a new idea—it's like living in a closet."

I looked down at her face, straining toward mine, at her pleading eyes, wide and clear now as they watched mine, and partly because she was getting under my skin, but also because I wanted her to stop talking, I said, "Sure, honey. We'll go."

"Tonight, Chris? You mean it? We'll go away?"

"Yeah, tonight. After—" She sighed and her eyes closed again.

"All right. Yes. After—" She relaxed into the crook of my arm and the fever started in me. She turned and buried her face in my arm. I felt her tremble slightly and then she looked up at me again. We kissed a long, hard, sweet kiss that drove through me, making a music you could never hear, only feel. But you knew it was there. You both knew.

She spoke muffledly into my arm. (…feel shut in…" she said.

She twisted her body and groped behind her for the door handle. I reached across and opened it. She pulled herself off my lap and climbed onto the ground. She turned from the car and ran across the clearing toward a clump of low trees, her dress fluttering and billowing behind her.

She stopped among the trees. There was grass, deep and cool. She sank down into it, gazing up at me. She shrugged free of the dress and held out her arms. I knelt beside her. Her hands touched my neck, moved along my back. I felt the music: the graceful, heady figures of Mozart, the plaintive, singing melody of Tchaikovsky, the surge of Beethoven, and then, drowning out all the rest, an insistent, throbbing beat—half jungle, half civilized…

CHAPTER 2

Hazel was asleep, her tangled hair dark against the pale grass, her body silver and gray shadows under the moon. Her breasts rose and fell gently with her breathing. The inner music had stopped and there was nothing now but silence, broken now and then by the chirping of crickets, the hoarse croaking of a frog. The grass was cool against my face as I turned to look at her.

I had felt calm and peaceful at first and I had slept for a while, easily, without dreams, but now I was jumpy. I raised myself slowly, easing my arm out from under Hazel's head, trying not to waken her, and groped for my clothes. I found the pint bottle in my coat pocket and drew it out. I uncapped it, took a long pull and felt the warmth of the whisky spread through me. While I was putting the bottle away again, I felt Hazel stir beside me and when I looked around, her eyes were watching me.

"Drink?" I said.

"No, darling."

I sat there for a while.

"Think we'd better go?" I said.

She stretched lazily, lifting her arms in the air.

"There's no hurry," she said. "We've got all the time in the world—now."

Then I remembered what I'd forgotten, what had been drowned in the music and the fire and the sleep that followed. We were going away together. Suddenly it didn't seem so crazy. It seemed all right. It seemed natural.

"Do you want to go home first?" I asked.

"There's nothing there I need," she said. "How about your hotel?"

"Two dirty shirts and a worn-out pair of shoes."

"We can get more shirts."

"Sure."

She stretched again, luxuriously in the deep grass. Slowly she got to her feet and began doing something with her hair. I watched her for a while—the good, full breasts, the clean, curving lines of her thighs. Pretty soon I reached out and caught her ankle. She smiled at me with her hands in her hair. I pulled her down beside me. Faintly and far off, the music started again.

Suddenly she stiffened in my arms. She raised her head, listening. I paused and listened too.

There was the sound of a car, a smooth motor purring far away, but coming closer.

After a minute I relaxed and pulled her close to me. "We're off the road," I said. "They'll go on by."

She pulled away, tense. My hand was on her thigh and I felt gooseflesh. The car came nearer, winding up the low hill, the way we had come into the clearing. Suddenly Hazel jumped to her feet, picked up her dress and began pulling it on. I got up too.

"What's the difference?" I said. "We're going away."

"The car," she said. "Somebody might recognize it. It's in plain sight."

"But listen—" The car was quite close now and we could see the waving glow of its headlights through the trees. We were only a few feet from the road. Hazel was struggling with her dress, fumbling at the buttons. She didn't seem able to work them. I began to dress. Some of her fear had got into me and my own fingers were trembling, but I made it. I buttoned my shirt, listening to the sound of the car, watching Hazel. And then the car stopped.

It had stopped close by. The light from the headlights was bright in the clearing. And then they went out and there was quiet. Hazel had given up trying to button her dress. I put my hand on her arm and she was trembling.

"Get hold of yourself," I whispered. "Some farmer. He'll go away."

She didn't seem to hear me. She stood, taut as an E-string on a fiddle, her dress fluttering slightly in the slow breeze, her head bent to one side.

I heard the click of a door latch, then nothing for a while. I stood still, feeling my own heart beat, feeling Hazel's panic as she stood, waiting.

A thin light probed the clearing and I heard footsteps in the grass, a small, whispering sound. The light went here and there, playing over the convertible and on the trees that surrounded the clearing. It advanced slowly toward the car. I touched Hazel again and she stiffened away from me.

My eyes worked, trying to blend the sharp flashlight beam with the moonlight, so I could see who it was. The moon was still bright enough to show that whoever had the light was big, was a man, but I couldn't make out any definite shape or features. Then he got to the convertible, turned his back to us and leaned in, flashing the light into the seat. I recognized him then—the "big bastard," the "pig," the "gorilla" who sometimes hung around the tavern. The husband.

I glanced at Hazel. She had opened her mouth wide. I reached over to cover it with my hand, but she twisted away and screamed. She screamed piercingly and in terror and the man at the convertible turned and flashed his light toward us.

She ran, stumbling a little in her haste, screaming all the way—toward the convertible, toward her husband. Her unbuttoned dress spread out behind her.

"Danny!" she screamed.

I took a couple of steps after her, then stopped as the meaning of it sank in. I felt hollow in the pit of my stomach. The sound of her screaming went through me like shock waves. She threw herself on him, her hands clutching at his coat lapels. I heard her moan softly, "Oh, Danny. Thank God you came."

I stood there near the trees, thirty feet away from him across the clearing and I couldn't think, couldn't move. I stood there while he played the flashlight over me slowly. He took plenty of time about it and when he finally spoke, his voice was low and hard, edged with a kind of gloating anticipation.

"Well, well," he said. "It's the piano player."

There wasn't a hell of a lot for me to say. Hazel was sobbing hysterically against his chest, and he pushed her away with one hand.

"This man give you some trouble, honey?" he said.

He played the light over her.

"Button up your dress," he said.

Obediently she did it. Her hands were steadier now. Bitterness drove words into my mouth.

"What's the matter, baby?" I said. "Lose your nerve?"

The flashlight swung back to cover me.

"Don't listen to him, Danny," she said. "Take me home. Please, now."

"Get in the car," he said.

She climbed into the convertible and slid behind the wheel. The flashlight beam was steady on me. His snotty voice came again.

"There's two ways to deal with this," he said. "One is my way—personal. The other is with the law. I think I'll give you some of both."

I still couldn't think of anything to say.

"Turn on the lights," he said.

"Please, Danny," Hazel said. "Let's just go home."

"Turn on the goddam lights!"

She switched on the headlights. They threw bright light into the clearing. I was standing at the edge of the light circle and Danny Boy was a big black shadow beside the car. The flashlight went off and he tossed it onto the seat of the convertible. He started toward me across the clearing. The contrast in light and dark made his shadow loom like a skyscraper, only with those thick, sloping shoulders he was a top-heavy skyscraper. He moved slowly, his feet shuffling through the grass.

I didn't have any choice. I wasn't brought up to be a fighter. I was brought up to play the piano. Besides, the only thing there had been to fight for was now cowering behind the wheel of a car, crying over her own spilt milk. I had nothing to do with this anymore. I was used to running. I was good at it. Even in the dark. Even in a strange countryside.

So I turned and ran, straight back into the trees, away from the lights and the convertible, away from Hazel. I heard Danny curse behind me as I broke and then his feet, heavy, pounding through the brush after me. I ran with my hands out in front to ward off the branches of trees. The moon was shut out here and there was no way to tell where I was going or what might turn up in front of me. But I saw the steel fence in time to turn and follow it, stooping, along the edge of an open field. The trees were on my left, and between the fence and the trees was a path three or four feet wide that was easy going—but I knew it would be just as easy for Danny. My breath was loud now and my heart pounded in my head and I couldn't tell whether he was behind me or not. If he knew about the fence he might have cut across to head me off.

That pulled me up and I grabbed a strand of the fence and stopped long enough to listen and look back, panting for breath. He wasn't behind me on the path. I sucked in air and strained, listening. For a while I didn't hear anything. I guessed he had stopped too. Then there was the sound of his running again. It came from off to my left and behind me among the trees. So he did know about the fence.

I started back slowly, walking carefully on the path, doubling back along the fence, listening as I went. The big ape went on, trying to head me off, and I slipped back along the fence, a little faster all the time, till I saw him come out of the trees to the fence. Then I ducked back into the woods myself and raced toward the clearing, where the headlights of the convertible still glowed. I hoped Danny Boy would thrash around long enough to give me three or four minutes.

Hazel was sitting behind the wheel of the convertible, staring around. I was in deep shadow and I knew she couldn't see me unless she turned out the car lights. Since her ever-loving husband had told her to turn them on, I doubted that she would dare to turn them off.

I walked quietly toward the rear of the car, skirting the clearing to keep out of the light. My eyes were on the redhead at the wheel and she didn't glance around. I moved faster, made a wide circle around the rear of the car and then approached it along the driver's side, walking on tiptoe. By the time I had reached the door she still hadn't looked around. But when I spoke her name softly she jumped straight up, jerked her head around and opened her mouth to scream. I clamped my hand over it, forcing her head back against the top of the seat.

"Listen," I said. "You wanted to run away. Now's your chance. I'm going to get in and you're going to drive."

Her eyes were wide. She moved her head, trying to get away from my hand over her mouth and I tightened the grip and pulled her around to face me again. I stuck my right hand in my coat pocket and pulled out the pint bottle.

"The next sound you hear," I said, "will be the top of this bottle breaking off. It won't hurt you if you behave yourself."

I clenched my teeth and banged the top of the bottle on the metal frame of the car top. It splintered away and what was left of the whisky spilled onto the car and splashed on my hand. I held the jagged end up where she could see it.

"Open the door," I said.

Her hand found the latch and it clicked. The door opened. I held the broken bottle two inches from her face and took my hand off her mouth.

"Stand up," I said.

She got on her feet, bending over the wheel, holding it to steady herself.

"I'm going to slide under you," I said. "Don't make me stab your beautiful behind with this bottle."

I slid onto the seat and across it to the other side. I put my hand on her arm and she sat down behind the wheel again.

"Get going," I said. "There's time."

"Chris—"

"Just get going."

She started the engine. She'd had it in reverse and the car jumped backward and stalled. She changed the gear, started it again. She had been sitting taut and stiff, her head up high, but suddenly she crumpled forward, her head fell onto the wheel and she began to cry.

"Oh, God," I said.

"I can't, Chris," she said, the words broken and indistinct. "I can't do it—I haven't got—"

"I know it," I said. "Just get me out of here. Now." Before I could react, she had opened the door and was scrambling out of the car. She pushed the door shut and stood with both hands on it, looking at me across the seat. "Take the car, Chris. Go ahead. Forget about me."

"Look, baby—"

"Take the car, Chris! It's yours. Only go away and don't come back. He'll kill you."

I didn't have time to argue. I slid back under the wheel, she crumpled up again, backing away from the car with her hands over her face.

"So long, baby," I said. "Have a happy life."

I don't think she heard me.

I jammed the thing into reverse and backed in a half-circle over the rough ground. The lights flashed on the edge of the clearing, the clump of trees where we'd been a short time before, and I saw Danny Boy come charging out. I gunned the car and twisted the wheel, heading for the road a few feet away. There was another car parked now just beyond the place where we'd turned off. The rear end partly blocked the narrow lane. The left rear fender of the convertible crumpled as I skinned by and twisted into the road. I didn't look back.

When I came out of the wooded area and looked across the fields I saw that it was getting light in the east. Straight ahead of me, in a shallow valley, the lights of the town still glowed feebly.

When you're in a panic and half your blood has turned to alcohol, you don't always think straight. As I plunged down toward town in the convertible I remembered two things in my hotel room. One was a five-dollar bill I'd tucked away under the mattress. The other was a pint bottle of whisky. I couldn't get them out of my mind. All I had in my pocket was three dollars and some change. Two of the dollars had come from Hazel. I wondered whether she'd got her money's worth.

I knew it would be silly to hang onto the car. They'd find me right away. I'd have to leave it, and not far from town. I figured that by the time Danny and the redhead got into the other car and got it turned around, I'd have enough head start for a quick stop.

All right. But that's the way I figured it out at the time.

I raced into the sleeping town toward the main street. It would be broad daylight in a few minutes. Two blocks from the hotel I slowed down and finally cut the engine. I turned the corner and stopped opposite the side entrance, where Hazel had picked me up. I wondered who had been watching us—who had tipped off the ape-man husband.

I went into the hotel and glanced at the desk. The clerk was asleep, as usual. I tiptoed to the stairs and went up two at a time. The window of my room was open and as I unlocked and opened the door I heard the roar of a car coming into town and then a sudden braking. I looked out the window. Danny's car was stopped at the corner and he was climbing out, moving toward the convertible. I ducked back from the window as he glanced up at the hotel.

So my time had run out. I couldn't remember where I'd hidden my bottle. On my way past the bed I slid my hand under the mattress, feeling for the five-dollar bill, but it wasn't there. I went on out into the hall.

At the rear end of the hall was a window giving on a fire escape. I went back there. The window was closed but unlocked. I raised it and stepped onto the rickety iron framework. It trembled under me. I went down the steps toward the alley that ran behind the building on the main street.

I walked fast, away from the street where I'd parked the convertible, toward the south end of town. Two blocks ahead of me the alley angled to the left and found its way back to the main street. From there I would have to cross the railroad tracks, get into the woodlands on the other side of town and head for the highway three miles beyond. It would be a long run, but it could work.

I came to the turn in the alley and moved along to the street. There was a red-brick building fronting on the main street and I made my way along it slowly to where I could look around the corner, back toward the hotel. I heard a freight train rumbling over the nearby tracks, but didn't think much about it.

The street and sidewalk were clear and I stepped out of the alley, and walked fast along the walk toward the tracks.

The freight wasn't going to stop. It had slowed to maybe thirty-five miles an hour and it looked like a long one.

I heard a quick shout behind me.

"There he is!"

I looked back and saw half a dozen men grouped in front of the hotel. One of them was Danny, the gorilla. They started after me along the walk.

The long freight blocked my path to the woods. I couldn't jump between the cars to the other side and I didn't have time to wait for it to pass. If I could catch it, I might get away. But it was speeding up now and I still had fifty yards to go to reach the tracks. I started to sprint, hearing the shouts behind me over the train's rattle. I heard a powerful car coming, first behind the shouts, then drowning them out as it passed the running men.

I didn't look back any more. I couldn't hear the crowd now because of the noise the train made. It was making good time and I forced myself to speed up as I came alongside, running on the gravel beside the ties. I reached for a ladder on a boxcar, but it came too fast and my hands tore loose before I could get a grip. The next car was an oil tanker and I leaped for the wooden catwalk, got one arm and a leg over it and held on, waiting for my bursting lungs to quiet down.

When I looked back, the mob that had chased me out of town was standing in the field, looking after the train. One, who looked like Danny, limped back toward them from the tracks. He looked as if he might have tried to grab the rattler too, and missed.

I lay still for a long time with my arm and leg hooked over the edge of the catwalk and the next time I looked back I couldn't see any of the town.

CHAPTER 3

The rattler didn't slow down. It just went on and on for what seemed like a week. Really, it was from early morning to dark evening, maybe thirteen hours. Not long on the inside of a train, but hell and all on the outside. I traveled almost as far up and down, bouncing, as I did forward. Where I was headed, I had no idea. I didn't even know the direction we were traveling.

My stomach growled with hunger and I needed a drink. My head ached from the battering of the long, rough ride. My eyelids were sandpaper. I was ready to get off. But the train wouldn't slow down. I finally made up my mind that I'd get off at the next town whether we slowed down or not. If I busted my head, then I wouldn't worry about my stomach and if I didn't bust it, maybe I could get something to eat.

A thick woodland loomed on the opposite side of the tanker and I inched around to have a look. We were following the course of a small river and the woods grew along the near bank. Up ahead, on the far bank, was a cluster of bright lights. They didn't look like the lights of a town. Pretty soon I saw a huge, slowly turning wheel and knew the lights belonged to a carnival.

The town was on the other side of the tracks, at least a mile ahead. The rattler showed no signs of even pausing and I got ready to jump when the lights came nearer.

The right-of-way had been cleared to a distance of about fifteen feet and most of it was gravel. But grass had grown up over some of it and the line of trees was less than twenty feet away. If I jumped far enough and hard enough I might be able to hit the grass when I fell. I crouched down on the narrow catwalk and braced myself for the shock.

I took a deep breath. And then the brakes went on. I felt the quick shock, heard the squeaking groans of the cars bumping together, the clanking couplings. Then it eased off and came back again and we had slowed to about twenty miles per hour.

That would make everything a lot easier. But the lights of the carnival were very close now and the town wasn't far off on the other side of the tracks and it was time to go.

I went. Even at the slower speed, I had to sprint hard to accommodate the momentum, but I didn't fall on my head. I made it to the grass in a hurry and slowed to a trot, then finally stopped. The brakes were on to stay now and slowly the long rattler ground to a stop. Far down toward the caboose a lantern swung beside the train, coming in my direction. I turned and walked into the trees toward the river.

The grass was high and damp around my ankles. It was dark among the trees and they were thick enough that the carnival lights threw no gleam. I heard the music of a calliope faintly. It didn't thrill me.

My stomach had begun to ache. I needed food. But even more I needed a drink. I could feel it spreading through me, the awful thirst that isn't really a thirst, but a painful, desperate hollowness in every part of you. To "drive a guy to drink" is more than a figure of speech. But the "drive" comes from inside yourself, brother, and once it gets started, it never lets up.

I glanced toward the carnival lights. That was maybe a place where I could get a drink and a meal for a few hours' work. I might even get a steady job.

Steady. I laughed to myself. Good and steady, I thought—till the next time I passed out—or ran into some redhead.

I turned in the direction of the lights and took a couple of steps. I stumbled over a rock. Somebody gasped. The sound came from within six feet of me. Without looking, I grabbed up the rock. It was the size of a small grapefruit. I straightened and swung around in the same motion, the rock poised in my right hand. The gasp came again and turned into a word.

"No!"

There was a girl crouched against a tree. Her feet were bare and white against the dark grass. She carried a small bundle under one arm.

I stood still, holding the rock, and we stared at each other.

She was maybe thirteen. Maybe twenty. She was crouched down so I couldn't be sure, but I guessed that if she stood up straight, she'd be around five feet two. Her small white face was ghostly against the dark trunk of the tree. Her legs were bare like her feet and the dress she wore was plastered wetly against her thighs. Her hair was long and wet and hung stringily down around her face. She was shivering.

"Where did you come from?" I asked.

She didn't answer, just crouched against the tree, staring at me. It was a stupid question anyway. Clearly she had come out of the river. If this was the beginning of an attack of D.T.'s, I was running right on schedule.

I tried to take it easy, but my voice came out harsh.

"I won't hurt you," I said.

She shifted the bundle across her body and held it under the other arm. Her face remained motionless and her eyes stared darkly out of it.

Finally she spoke and her voice was flat, dull, without life or spark. It was a grown-up voice coming out of a little girl's face.

"They didn't send you—to get me?"

"I just got off that train," I said, jerking my head back toward the tracks.

"Where is it going?" she said.

"I don't know. I got off because I didn't know."

She straightened a little against the tree trunk and pushed some of the wet hair away from her face.

"It's going away," she said.

"Any minute now."

I had begun to shake. I held tight to the rock, trying to keep a grip on something—anything.

Her face had moved now. She was staring past me toward the tracks. I glanced that way, saw the swinging red light of the brakie's lantern returning along the train, moving toward the rear.

The little-girl face turned back to me.

"Will you help me?" she said. "I have to get on that train."

"I just got off the goddam thing," I said.

When she'd asked for help a flicker of hope had risen in her voice. But it didn't last.

"All right," she said dully and moved away.

She walked toward the line of trees that bordered the right-of-way, stumbling as she went. She carried the bundle against her left hip. She didn't look strong enough to make it as far as the train, thirty feet ahead.

I caught up with her, put my left hand on her shoulder. There was a single line of trees between us and the track.

"Wait," I said. "Don't try it till it starts up. They might haul you off."

She stopped, staring ahead toward the train.

"As soon as it begins to roll," I said, "head for one of those empty box cars. You'll have to jump to get inside."

"All right," she said. She didn't look at me.

From far ahead came the sound of the bell, wavering in the night. Then the whistle, sharp and shrill, and out from under the whistle, the new head of steam.

The noise from the train had drowned out the approach. The girl and I heard the footsteps shuffling through the grass at the same time. They stopped when we whirled around.

The guy who stood there, five feet from us, was as big as a boxcar. His shoulders were wide, thick and sloping. His hands hung beside him like a couple of sides of beef. He wore a dark hat pulled down over his forehead. His face was smashed and swollen. If he had a neck, it wasn't visible.

The girl didn't gasp. She didn't move. She was frozen. Although we weren't touching, I could feel the tension in her.

"Where in hell did you think you was goin'?" the big one asked.

The girl didn't answer. I heard the couplings grind as the long train tightened up, ready to roll.

The ape man had eyes only for the girl. He didn't even seem to know I was there.

"You ain't goin' nowhere," he said.

He said it the way you might say, "It looks like rain." It was a simple statement of fact. Only he had the beef to back up his statements.

I glanced at the girl. She seemed tinier than before, with his huge bulk towering over her. She clutched the bundle in both arms, her shoulders hunched forward, her white face a mask of terror and defeat. Behind us there was the grating rumble of the freight as it began to roll.

The big bruiser took a step toward the girl. She made a sound, a low, moaning sound like a sick animal makes to warn you off. It cut me inside, as if I had swallowed a razor blade. The guy reached toward her with both of his beefy hands. She seemed to shrink down into the ground, though actually she didn't move. The sound she had made was still slicing at my lungs.

I swung my right arm up and over and let go of the rock. It struck him in the side of the head and the noise it made was about the same as if I had hit the frame wall of a house. He twisted his face toward me, as if he had noticed me for the first time. His mouth was open. Then he fell, straight and stiff to the ground, like a tree might fall. The rock lay on the ground near his feet.

I knelt beside him and went through his pockets. In the right hip pocket was a worn, smooth wallet. I looked inside. There was a ten, a twenty and a couple of singles. I took them out. Something pulled at my sleeve. I looked up and the girl was staring down at me.

"The train," she said. "It's moving."

"Yeah," I said.

I wasn't through. He had some other pockets. One of them, his left coat pocket, bulged out around a large, smooth hump. I pulled it out. It was a pint bottle, labeled straight bourbon, and it was half full.

The girl pulled at me again. I straightened up, shoving the bottle into my coat pocket as we moved toward the tracks. She was ahead of me and when we got onto the right-of-way, beyond the trees, I grabbed her arm and pulled her back. The rattler was picking up speed, but it was still crawling and we had time to do it right.

"Wait for a boxcar," I said, "and then follow me."

She waited. The bottle was heavy and reassuring in my pocket. Let's not break it, I thought. For God's sake, let's not break it!

An empty boxcar loomed three or four cars down, the open door inviting.

"Come on," I said and trotted diagonally across the right-of-way, looking back to measure the distance.

She came right along, almost stumbling over my heels. I looked back at her once and her white face was reaching out toward me. She wasn't looking at the train, just at me.

The empty was one car behind when I got to the ties. I pulled her up even with me, then pushed her ahead.

"Don't run too fast," I said. "When the door catches up with you, throw in your bundle."

She ran along, limping on her bare feet over the loose gravel of the roadbed. I was close behind her. From the corner of my eye I saw the open door of the empty pulling up on my right. I waited till the front edge had passed me and then shouted to her.

"Now! The bundle!"

She tossed the bundle into the open door and I speeded up, ran close behind her, synchronizing my steps with hers.

"Put your hands flat on the floor," I said.

She did it, running awkwardly now to keep up with the train. I got my hands on her upper thighs in back.

"Jump!" I said.

She jumped feebly. I pulled up on her thighs. She bent her knees and for a moment I carried her full weight, running. Then I boosted her up hard and she fell forward into the car, rolling away from the door.

My heart was pounding in my chest. The train rolled faster every second. I put my hands flat on the floor of the car, jumped up, locked my elbows and hung there for a few seconds, trying to catch my breath. Slowly I pulled up one knee, got it firm on the floor, hunched myself up and fell in beside the girl.

CHAPTER 4

I lay still, sucking air in big gasps, waiting for the pain in my chest to subside. I got the bottle out of my pocket, twisted the cap off, wiped the mouth with my sleeve and tipped it up. The warmth of the whisky relaxed my throat, spread through my chest, my stomach, filtered down through my belly, even my legs. I had another. My condition began to slide back to what, for me, was normal. I held up the bottle and peered at it. There were still three good shots left. The hand that held it shook only a little. I put the bottle back in my pocket.

The girl lay still beside me. Her head rested on one out-flung arm and her other arm lay beside it. Her knees were drawn up. Her dress had slid halfway up her bare thigh and still clung to her skin. I reached over and put my hand on the stuff of her dress. It was still very wet.

I got on my knees, found a packet of matches in my pocket, struck one and leaned down over her bare feet. They were mostly black on the bottom and corrugated, as if she had gone barefoot most of her life. But there were two or three broken places on each sole and they were bleeding slowly.

I found a handkerchief, none too clean, and reached for the bottle. I held it up, hesitating. I studied the bottle and swore softly to myself. I had played a sucker's role practically every minute for the last twenty-four hours and maybe it was time to stop. Any time a lush like me began to think of washing a girl's feet in hard liquor—good or bad—the world stopped moving.

I unscrewed the cap again, held the handkerchief against the mouth of the bottle and tipped it carefully. Just as carefully I held it upright while I applied the damp handkerchief to the sole of her right foot, dabbing at the places I could see were bleeding.

Her foot jerked spasmodically. I looked around and found her raised up, supporting herself on her hands, staring at me. I held the bottle toward her so she could see it.

"Alcohol," I said.

I don't think she heard me. She leaned there, watching me and her feet held still while I dabbed the precious fluid on the torn spots. When I finished I held the bottle up again and I felt better. The level was almost the same as when I had put it away the first time. You get so you can judge levels with great accuracy.

She was staring at the bottle as I put it away in my pocket again, but I pretended not to notice. I didn't feel good about it, but I thought I would feel worse if I offered it to her and she took it. I shoved it down deep in my coat pocket, turned and sat up with my arms around my knees, looking out the door of the swaying car.

Pretty soon I felt her beside me. She sat the same way I did, her arms wrapped around her drawn-up knees. We started around a slow curve and she fell against me, then straightened up right away. Her face turned to me and she said something I couldn't hear.

In the open doorway with the clatter of the wheels and the heavy squeak of the couplings beating our ears, everything had to be shouted. If she wanted conversation, we'd have to move farther inside.

I stood up and reached out my hand. She took it and I pulled her up to her feet. We stood, swaying, looking at each other and finally I took her arm and led her back into the car, toward the front of the train. The noise let up.

"Can't hear anything over there," I said.

She looked up at me with her little white face. "I said, 'Thank you'," she said.

I nodded. "I said, 'Don't mention it.'"

It was real smart talk.

We straightened out from the long curve and she lurched again. I held out my hand and she fell against it. Her ribs were prominent and she felt like skin and bones, but her breast was large and firm under the wet cloth. When she was steady on her feet I dropped my hand.

"Better take those wet clothes off," I said.

"All right," she said.

The air blowing in from outside was cool but not bitter. I took off my coat and held it out to her. Then I remembered the whisky bottle and grabbed it out of the pocket. I walked over near the door and set the bottle down on the floor. I was still holding the coat. When I turned back to give it to her, she was pulling the dress off over her head. I stopped where I was for a couple of seconds and then went on over and handed her the coat. From what I could see of it in the dark interior of the car, her figure was good. But I wasn't much interested. I was hungry and I was getting thirsty again and I still felt like a sucker. I figured that she would get along all right, now that she'd got started and I could ditch the freight in the morning. At the rate we were going, we'd be out of the state in a few hours.

She slipped into the coat and buttoned it in front. It dropped almost to her knees and her hands disappeared when she let the sleeves hang straight. She put the ends of the sleeves together in front of her and hunched her shoulders forward and I saw that she was still cold.

It occurred to me that I hadn't inspected the other end of the car. I walked back there, past the open door. The sweet smell of alfalfa drifted into my nostrils and at first I thought it came from outside. Then I stumbled against a thick, hard-packed stack of it, reached down and found a bale under my hands. I struck a match and looked at it.

There was about half of it still intact. The wires had been broken and the part that had been used was scattered over the floor. I started to kick the loose stuff into a pile. After a while I was kicking it into two piles.

"Hey!" I called to the girl.

She came slowly toward me, hunched into my coat, her hands still out of sight in the sleeves.

I pointed to the piles of hay on the floor.

"Next best thing to an innerspring mattress," I said.

A little smile flickered at the corners of her mouth. It was the first one. It made her look almost pretty, in spite of the still wet, stringy hair, the paleness of her face and the outlandish costume.

I lay down on one of the piles and tested. It was deep enough. It cut down the bouncing of the car and it was warm.

The girl watched me. I indicated the other pile and she went to it slowly, knelt, tried it with her hand and then lay down on it, on her back, her white face turned to me. She smiled again. She was still cold. Every few seconds a tremor would run through her from head to toe and she would hunch into the coat.

I got up and went to the other end of the car and picked up my bottle and the little bundle she'd been carrying before we got on. The bundle was wrapped in an old-fashioned oil slicker, tied with binding twine. I carried the stuff back to where she was lying on the pile of hay.

"Got any dry clothes in here?" I said, holding up the bundle.

She shook her head.

"Just the raincoat," she said, "and two sandwiches."

My mouth filled.

"Sandwiches?"

"Are you hungry?"

"Since you ask me—" I said.

She reached up for the bundle and I handed it down to her. She unrolled the slicker and came up with a battered paper sack. Out of it she took a sandwich of white bread with what smelled like boiled ham inside. She offered it to me, and I took a bite. It was a little damp, a little ragged around the edges and the bread had been packed into a thin, tasteless wad of dough. But it was the first food I'd had for more than eighteen hours and it went down all right.

The girl ate about half of hers and put the rest back in the sack. She still shivered with cold and I kicked at the bale, loosening the alfalfa in it, and started to cover her with it, piling it on thick. She lay still on her back, her face looking up at me as I worked. Finally there was nothing but her face showing out of the pile of hay.

The sandwich was like a stone in my stomach and I took a swig of the whisky to dissolve it. I looked over and the girl was watching me. There were two shots left. I would want another before going to sleep and I'd need one to straighten me out in the morning. I knew that as soon as the bottle was empty, the pain would set in, the desperation.

If she had looked away from me, I think I might have held out. But the little white face didn't move. Her eyes stared darkly, intently at me out of the pile of hay.

I offered her the bottle.

"No, thank you," she said.

I was torn up inside and my voice came out gruff and harsh.

"Better take some. You got chilled."

I held it closer.

The pile of hay moved and her hand came out of it and closed around the bottle. I looked away while she drank it. When I looked back, she was holding it out to me. I took it and replaced the cap. She had only sipped at it. The level hadn't dropped more than an eighth of an inch. I stashed the bottle away in the alfalfa, near where I planned to put my head.

I looked over at the girl and found her eyes were closed. She lay very still under the hay. I didn't see any more shivering.

I got myself some more loose stuff out of the bale and stretched out, pulling the hay over me to my chin. The air was colder and would get steadily colder until dawn. But the alfalfa was warm and there was plenty of it.

It took a long time for me to relax. Finally I pulled the bottle out of the hay under my head and took a swig. I put the cap back on and shook it to see whether there was any left. There was a little. I stuck the bottle back into the hay. After a while I went to sleep.

I woke once before dawn and something had changed. A rough edge of cloth rubbed at my neck. It was my own coat, the one I'd given the girl when she took off her wet dress. I looked over at the other pile of hay.

Only her small white face showed in the dark.

It was the lurch and jarring as the train slowed that woke me the next time. Daylight spilled into the car. The brakes went off, came on again, went off once more and came on to stay. I got up from the pile of hay, dusted off my coat and put it on. I found the bottle and stuck it in my pocket. I walked to the door and looked out.

The sun was rising toward the rear end of the train and was out of sight from where I stood. That meant we were traveling northwest. I leaned out and looked ahead but saw no sign of a town. There was a high water tower and a small yellow frame building near it, but no other buildings. I figured we must be on the B. & O. line, probably heading for Chicago.

We were crawling along, about to stop, and I knew it would be smart to get off and out of sight before the brakie came to throw me off. I looked back at the girl, still asleep on the pile of hay. I didn't want to be connected with her. I had enough to look out for in myself. But I couldn't walk away from her.

I walked back and shook her a little. She turned her head toward me and opened her eyes slowly. It was the first good look I'd had at her face. It was pale and thin and there were heavy circles under her eyes. But I could imagine it being pretty, given some care and the right kind of makeup.

Her eyes blinked at the sunlight and she pulled away from my hand.

"Better get off now," I said. "We're about to stop."

She blinked again. Her eyes were deep brown.

"All right," she said.

I picked up her dress from the remains of the bale of hay. It was dry now. It looked like a dress that you might buy in a variety store for a dollar ninety-eight. I tossed it to her and walked away to the door. I couldn't figure out what to do about her. I hated to think of her getting thrown into some stinking small-town jail or winding up with the ugly bruiser I'd cooled with the rock. But then again, I wasn't Robin Hood. I hadn't asked her any questions, because I hadn't wanted to know the answers. My own story was sad enough. I didn't need any more. I tried to tell myself she'd be all right now. If the train was headed for Chicago and she could stay with it, maybe she could find what she wanted in the city. If not, then she could keep on running—like me.

I pulled the bottle out of my pocket. There was a good shot left. Only one, but now I had money. I drained off the last of it and felt warm and calm in the sunlight. I threw the bottle into the end of the car.

The train had stopped. The land sloped in an open meadow from the edge of the right-of-way to a river fifty yards beyond. Willows grew thickly along the river banks. I glanced out the door toward the end of the train. A brakeman was climbing down from the caboose. I looked around and the girl was standing close behind me, clutching the wadded-up slicker in both arms.

I jumped down onto the gravel roadbed. The girl came to the edge of the door and hesitated, lifting one bare foot, then putting it down again. I remembered her torn, bleeding feet. I reached up and she crouched into my arms and I let her down easily. She winced when her feet struck the hot pebbles.

I picked her up. She couldn't have weighed over ninety pounds. She held the slicker tightly and looked into my face as I carried her into the meadow toward the river.

Her eyes were big and dark and frank, like a child's eyes. But she couldn't be a child—not with those breasts.

Halfway across the meadow I stopped to look back. The brakeman had reached our car. He was standing by the open door, looking in our direction. When he saw me looking at him he lifted his hand and waved it in a pushing motion, telling me to keep moving. That was good. He didn't want to talk to me, he just wanted me to stay off the train. We were probably in Indiana by now and maybe they hadn't bothered to send out an alarm for me from that tank town.

I looked at the girl in my arms and grinned a little.

"We better not get back on that one," I said.

She just looked at me out of those eyes.

It was hot in the sun, but among the trees it was cool and the deep grass under foot was soft and damp. I let her down and we walked onto the soft mud bank of the river. She dug her toes into the mud and squished her feet around in it. It must have felt pretty good.

She looked back at me and smiled slowly, a half-wistful, half-frightened smile. Her dark hair fell in a tangle around her face. The pale skin had smudge spots here and there, on her forehead, on one cheek, on her narrow chin.

"I feel dirty all over," she said.

"Freight trains are dirty," I said. "I'm sorry I don't have any soap."

She smiled a little more.

"Anyway, we have plenty of water," she said.

Before I could catch her whole meaning, she had taken the hem of her wrinkled, flimsy dress and pulled it up over her head. She freed her arms from it and tossed the dress back onto the grass. She seemed to have no sense of shame or embarrassment as she stood there naked at the edge of the water. But she wasn't giving an exhibition either. It all happened like a completely natural thing.

Why not? I thought. She wants to go into the water. She doesn't want to get the dress wet again. She takes it off.

She waded into the river and I watched the water rise slowly around her, traveling up her thin calves, hiding her knees, her slender thighs, her hips that seemed wider than they should have been to fit her near-skinny figure. Finally she turned to look at me. The water came just to the under curves of her breasts. They seemed to float in front of her.

She dipped her arms into the water and threw some of it up into her face. She bent her head, wet her hair and scrubbed at it with her hands. When she straightened again she was beckoning to me with both hands.

"It feels good," she called. "You ought to try it."

I could see that it felt good. I could use a little scrubbing myself. I was getting anxious to push on to a town, find a liquor store and maybe a new job. But I'd have a better chance at the job if I washed off some of the road dirt first.

I took off my shoes and socks, coat and shirt and pants. I hesitated. Then I laughed. The old inhibitions die hard, I thought. She didn't have any. Why should I? I found myself wondering where she'd lost them. I went ahead and stripped down to the skin and splashed into the water.

It did feel good. I hadn't had a good swim for a long time. I struck out for the opposite bank, taking it easy and slow and I felt good when I got there. But the current had carried me downstream a few yards and it was hard work bucking it to get back to her. I came up, sputtering and coughing, in front of her. Her eyes were wide and awestruck.

"You can swim," she said.

"Millions of people can swim."

"Not me," she said. "They'd never let me."

"Who wouldn't?"

"They," she said and looked away.

I scrubbed myself as well as I could, wishing I had some soap. The river water was none too clean, but it was all right if I didn't stir it up too much.

I guided her over the slippery mud of the bank and we picked up our clothes and walked back among the trees. We found a clearing where enough sun came through to dry us and the grass was clean and dry. She lay down on the grass, on her back, her arms flung out, her eyes closed against the sun. Lying there, relaxed, her skin not so taut over her bones, she looked less skinny, more like a woman, curving and graceful. The sun or the exertion, or both, had faintly reddened her cheeks and there was some pink now to soften the stark whiteness of her face.

I stretched out beside her and looked at the patches of blue sky that showed among the leaves overhead. I felt relaxed and comfortable, no fluttering in the stomach, no shaking, no hollowness of hunger-thirst. It might have been a good sign, but I knew better than to believe it.

You couldn't get over it that way. You could relax once in a while, for a little while, and then the memories came crawling back. You had always deliberately drowned the memories and as long as you lived in the foggy, half-real world, under the anesthesia of drink, they would remain submerged. But when you came out of it, as your mind cleared, the memories rose to the surface, slowly at first, dull and formless, and then faster and faster and sharper and took full possession, stabbing at you, twisting in your head, your chest, your stomach. It all came back, the old pain, the hates, the fears. Every casual glance from a stranger was hostile, threatening. Every suggestion became a persecution. You got nailed to a cross a hundred times every hour. And so you reached for the glass and began to drown them again, the hateful, twisting memories out of the dark and dingy past.

I knew it would happen again, as always, even here in a sunlit grove by a quiet river, without problems, without hunger. A few minutes of peace, of warmth and contentment, and then I would begin to go taut again, to thrash about in my mind, struggling against awareness, dodging the pain, aching again for the anesthetic, the liquid fire with the horrible taste that brought quick and easy relief.

The girl spoke, her quiet voice a cymbal crash out of silence.

"Thank you for helping me," she said.

"It's all right," I said.

After a moment she said, more softly than before, "Do you want me now?"

She asked it flatly, without emotion or even expression. Each word had exactly the same tone and timber as every other.

I raised myself on one elbow and looked at her. The pattern of the leaves above us made half-toned lights and shadows over her white body. She looked at me, her dark eyes as flat and expressionless as her voice. When I looked into her eyes she turned her head away. When I didn't move to her, she looked back at me.

"How old are you?" I asked.

She looked startled, as if she hadn't thought about it for a long time.

"Twenty-one," she said.

I put my hand on her, on her breast. Her skin was cool and still damp from the river. There was no response in it to my touch. She lay still, not looking at me, waiting. My hand had asked a question and she had made no answer. None whatever, of fear, of passion, of pleasure or pain. I removed my hand and lay back on the ground.

"No," I said. "I haven't done anything for you. Anyway, that's not something you can earn."

It was her turn to raise up and look at me. When I met her gaze there was something new in it, a kind of shy curiosity. She moved her arm up and partially concealed her breasts.

"What's your name?" I said.

She hesitated.

"They called me Dolores."

That was the second time she had mentioned some mysterious people known as "they."

"The big guy that I hit with the rock," I said. "Was he one of—*them?*"

She nodded slightly.

"There were three of them. He was her husband—Madeleine's. Then there was another girl. Her name was Mitzi."

"And they called you Dolores?"

"Yes."

"But Dolores isn't your real name?"

Again she hesitated.

"No."

"All right. You don't have to tell me your real name."

Her voice was a bare whisper when she said, "My real name is Constance—Constance Jordan."

It didn't mean anything to me.

"All right, Connie," I said. "My name is Chris."

Her eyes had that flat look again. Her arm fell away from her breasts.

"You don't believe me," she said.

"Why shouldn't I believe you?" I said. "What's so special about the name Constance Jordan?"

She sat up slowly and reached for the wadded-up slicker that lay on the grass beside her. Slowly, hopelessly she unrolled it and dug around in it with her fingers. Finally she found what she wanted and held it out to me, her eyes still flat and empty.

It was a fragile, smudged scrap of newsprint, ragged along the edges, the print barely legible in the folds. It had been clipped from a Los Angeles daily. A part of the name of the paper ran vertically alongside the news story in the margin. Although it was datelined less than a year before, the paper was already beginning to yellow.

I held it carefully and read it. There was a fourteen-point, two-line head:

JORDAN ESTATE FINALLY SETTLED

Los Angeles, Calif., August 9, 1951.—Executors for the estate of Philip M. Jordan, millionaire oil man and financier, announced today that a final settlement has been made of the estate after nearly eight years of investigation and delay.

Bulk of the fortune goes to Jordan's older daughter, Jean. A younger daughter, Constance, was kidnapped at the age of thirteen, on March 28, 1943. Final settlement of the estate was made possible by a recent decision in local courts declaring Constance legally dead.

Believed to have been seized in the street while she was returning home from school, Constance Jordan was never found. A telephoned demand for ransom of fifty thousand dollars was met and Philip Jordan, personally and alone, kept the rendezvous at which the money was to be delivered and the girl returned unharmed. He was met, as he stated afterward, by a man and woman. When he demanded to see his daughter before turning over the money, the man slugged him unconscious. A three-year search by police and the F.B.I. failed to locate the girl. Jordan was unable positively to identify the man and woman who met him from hundreds of police photos shown him. He died within three months of the kidnapping.

Under the provisions of Jordan's will, the two sisters were to divide the estate equally between them when they came of age. With the younger daughter declared dead, the older girl receives the entire legacy. Many girls have come forward during the past seven years claiming to be the missing Constance Jordan. But although exhaustive investigation was made in every case, each claim was found to be fraudulent. Identification of Constance hinged on certain bodily markings the nature of which, "for obvious reasons," was never made public. She had never been fingerprinted.

I handed the fragile clipping back to her. I remembered more about it now. I had been in Los Angeles at the time of the kidnapping of the Jordan girl. I remembered the tense headlines during the first days and the photos of the stricken father. I remembered how the story had died out as news and how it was revived every few weeks, as another girl stepped up to claim the fortune.

The girl beside me had put the clipping away somewhere in the folds of the slicker. She didn't look at me anymore. She sat with her arms around her drawn-up knees, staring toward the river.

"What makes you think you'll have any more luck than those other girls who tried it?" I said.

Her answer was simple and direct.

"Because I am Constance Jordan," she said.

When I didn't answer, she turned slowly and looked at me, her eyes alive again, pleading, intense.

"Will you help me some more?" she said. "I've got to get back. If you'll help me, I can pay you when we get there."

Something in my face must have told her I thought she was dreaming, because her eyes went flat and hopeless again.

"You don't believe it," she said. "But I'm Constance Jordan. I remember everything that happened. I remember that day, coming home from school. And everything after that. I remember!"

Her desperate hunger to be believed took hold of me. I couldn't believe it yet. But she was getting under my skin.

I got to my feet.

"We'd better find a town," I said.

She looked up at me for a long time, her eyes doubtful, still hopeless. Then she reached for her flimsy dress, pulled it over her head, stood up and straightened it over her hips. She wadded the slicker up into a bundle and tucked it under her arm. We started off.

CHAPTER 5

We came to a town a couple of miles up the river. It was a lot like the one I'd been run out of, except that it was a little bigger. The main street crossed the river at the south end of town and became a country road on the other side. There were five or six blocks of stores, markets and commercial buildings and the residential streets stretched east and west on each side. There were a lot of trees.

As soon as we got onto the sidewalk, Connie (I hadn't yet started calling her that in my mind) had trouble. The cement was hot under the sun and it must have been torture for her to put her feet on it. Whenever there was a stretch of grass near the walk, we moved over on that. I began looking for a place to get her some shoes.

I found it within a block and a half, a variety store. It was run-down-looking and the windows were cluttered with junk. But the prices were low and the merchandise looked wearable. I reached into my pocket and pulled out my money. With the thirty-two bucks I'd lifted from the ape man and what I'd found in the kitty the night before, I had thirty-six dollars and forty cents. I gave Connie twenty.

"You'll need some shoes and another dress and some stuff," I told her. "I hope you can get it with this."

She hesitated, but she didn't argue.

"Where are you going?" she asked.

"I'm going up the street. I'll meet you back here in half an hour."

"All right."

She went into the store, clutching the money in one hand, holding the slicker in a wad under her other arm.

I walked up the street till I found a package store and went in and bought a fifth of cheap stuff. I asked the clerk about the situation when it came to taverns or cocktail lounges and he mentioned the Blackstone Hotel and a beer joint called the Green Lantern. There's one in every town.

The Blackstone Hotel was quiet and well run. It reached up eight stories high and the lobby was decorated in a conservatively modern style, with comfortable, expensive chairs and love seats. In the corner opposite the lobby desk was a sign reading: zephyr room, with an arrow pointing down. At the desk, the clerk told me I would find the manager in the cocktail lounge. The manager's name was Art Rose.

I crossed the lobby and started down, carrying my paper sack with the bottle in it. The stairs were wide with a banister in the middle. At the bottom, straight ahead, was a set of double doors and a sign over them reading zephyr room. One of the doors stood open and I walked in.

The room was small and intimate. There were twenty-five or thirty cocktail tables grouped around a dime-sized dance floor, and twelve stools at the curving bar. At one end was a jukebox. There was a platform beside the jukebox, big enough for a small upright or maybe a baby grand. But there was nothing on it now.

A porter was cleaning up. Chairs were stacked on the tables and he was going over the carpeted floor with a vacuum cleaner. The manager was behind the bar, fooling around with the cash register. I went over there and sat down on a stool.

"Mr. Rose?" I said.

He turned and looked at me. He was heavy in the face, wider at the jaws than up above. He had a dark complexion and a very black beard, which still showed, even though you could see he had shaved within the last few minutes. He wasn't unfriendly and he wasn't cordial either. He had that no-nonsense, let's-get-down-to-brass-tacks look. None of his movements was hurried or nervous, but he kept busy all the time. After he had looked at me he went back to work at the register.

"Yes?" he said.

"I play the piano," I said.

"Uh-huh?"

"I'd like to play it for you."

He didn't look around.

"That's a nice idea," he said, "but I don't have any piano for you to play."

"Maybe we could find one."

He looked around then.

"You're talking about playing the piano in here, in the cocktail lounge?"

"That's right."

He glanced around the room as if he were thinking about it, and then shook his head and turned back to the register.

"Afraid not," he said. "We've got a jukebox. I had an organ for a while, but nobody seemed to like it much."

"Yeah," I said. "People get tired of organs. I'm talking about a piano."

He finished with the register and slammed it shut. He stooped over and began to check the stock on the shelves under the back bar. Then he turned and leaned on the bar.

"I don't think we can use you," he said. "The room doesn't do enough business to warrant it."

"Maybe I could increase the business," I said. "Do they come to dance?"

"Not much dancing," he said. "They come in for a couple of drinks, maybe after a show or something. Play the jukebox. It's a quiet place."

"How long since you've had it filled up?"

"It fills up twice a year," he said. "Once at Christmas and once at the end of the football season."

It was time to give him the pitch, such as it was. I didn't know why I was doing it. It would have been easier to take my bottle and sit down in the shade somewhere till it was gone and then to get moving. But there was a girl down the street, waiting for me, and I kept having the idea I had to take her something, even if it was only a job.

"I wouldn't guarantee to keep it filled up for you," I said, "every night. But I've seen it happen—a bar picks up a lot with a little music and a real live guy to play it."

"I don't know—"

"Some people like to sing," I said, pressing it. "The old familiar tunes. If you've got somebody who can knock them out, you've got somebody they go for."

"Can't have anything rowdy," he said.

"I'm not talking about rowdy. Just the sweet old tunes, like 'Let the Rest of the World Go By,' 'Tie Me to Your Apron Strings Again,' 'A Pretty Girl Is Like a Melody.' You know what I mean."

"I can get a kid in high school to play those tunes," he said.

"I play other things too."

"Like what?"

"Where can I audition?"

He shrugged. He didn't like being sold, but he was softening up.

"Music store across the street," he said.

He walked out from behind the bar and I followed him up the stairs and across the lobby, still lugging my bottle. We went into the bright sunlight and across the street to a placed called the Westbrook Music Company. Westbrook must be the name of the town, I thought.

Inside there was sheet music in racks. There were some instruments, from drums to tubas; phonographs, television sets and in the back a few pianos. A sign said pianos for sale or rent. There were four spinets, brand-new, an old, ornate upright, a couple of small grands and a studio upright, somewhat beat up. But it was finished in oak, so it didn't look too bad.

An old guy with white hair walked up to us.

"Hello, Art," he said.

"Bert," said Rose, "we'd like to borrow the use of one of your pianos for a few minutes."

"Help yourself," the white-haired guy said.

We went back to where the pianos were and Rose found a chair and sat down. I stuck my bottle under the keyboard of one of the spinets and looked around for something that would be in tune. One of the grands was in pretty good shape and I struck a few chords on it and finally went to the studio upright, hoping.

It was in tune.

I sat down and ran through a little of my standard repertoire: 'Sweet Lorraine,' 'King Peter Stomp' and a few bars of 'Honky Tonk Train.' Now and then I glanced at Rose. His face was dead as yesterday's glass of beer.

I swung into some of the familiar tunes I'd mentioned to him, playing them soft and straight. When I got to "Harvest Moon" I glanced at him again and his finger was tapping on the arm of the chair. So I stopped. If not now, I thought, then never.

His eyes looked at me, but his mind was off somewhere by itself. There was no way to tell what he was thinking. Finally he said, "You play any other type of music?"

"What do you mean?" I said. "Like Chopin, Beethoven—stuff like that?"

"That's what I mean."

I had hoped he wouldn't ask that.

"Yeah, I can play it," I said then. "But in a tavern or lounge—you don't get much call for it."

"Can't tell," he said, "in a place like mine."

I hesitated some, then turned back to the keyboard.

"O.K.," I said. "It's been a long time."

I played the Minute Waltz. I had to fake like hell to get through it. When I finished there was a hard lump in my stomach. I glanced over at the place where I'd stashed my bottle. My tongue was dry and stiff. I played the opening bars of the B-Flat Minor Concerto by Tchaikovsky, then I played some of the Warsaw Concerto—flashy stuff, like they would ask for in a bar if they got the urge for it. Finally, for contrast, I gave him an Arabesque by Debussey. This time when I stopped, the sweat stood cold on my head and I could feel it dripping down my sides under my shirt. It was hard to swallow. Truly, it had been a long time.

Rose was looking into space again with that inscrutable expression that I was coming to hate. I rubbed my damp palms together and looked at my bottle and thought, the hell with it. I don't want the goddam job anyway.

The paper sack with the bottle in it was drawing me like a magnet. I wondered whether I could reach it without getting up and attracting a lot of attention. I had started to reach for it, bending out on the piano bench, when he spoke to me.

"How much would it cost me?" he said.

He'd snapped it at me fast and caught me off balance. I stalled some.

"Well—I'm not likely to run into union problems here," I said. "I could get by all right for—let's say board and room and seventy-five a week."

He just laughed. He laughed silently, opening his mouth and throwing his head back, but no sound.

"I wish I could take seventy-five a week out of it for myself," he said.

"Well, let's haggle," I said.

He didn't answer right away. He looked around the store and found the old white-haired guy that ran it.

"How much would this piano cost me—to rent?" he asked.

The old guy scratched his chin.

"For the Zephyr Room?"

"That's right."

A twinkle came into the old man's eyes.

"Tell you what," he said, "I'll let you have it, as a personal favor, for eight dollars. You pay the cartage on it both ways."

"O.K.," said Rose.

"Shall I call it a deal?" asked the old man.

"Not yet."

Rose looked at me.

"The seventy-five a week is out," he said. "If you'll do it for room and board and whatever you can get 'em to put in the kitty, I'll try you out for a week."

"Make it room and board for myself and my wife," I said. "Board includes food and drink."

"Drink a lot, do you?" he said.

"Not too much."

"Where's your wife?"

"Down the street, shopping."

The "wife" thing was a spur-of-the-moment thought. I didn't expect the girl to be around for long, if at all. But it would give us something to negotiate about after she left.

Rose studied me for a while. Then he said, "There's a room with a double bed in the basement. You'll have to furnish your own maid service."

"Is it a clean room?"

"It will be clean by five o'clock this afternoon," he said.

He had made a deal, but I couldn't let him think I was falling in head first.

"For one week," I said, "you have hired yourself a piano player. After the first week we talk it over."

"O.K.," he said and held out his hand.

We shook on it. Rose turned to the white-haired proprietor.

"Send it over this afternoon. Tell 'em to put it on the platform by the jukebox. O.K.?"

"All right, Art," the man said.

Rose turned and started out of the store. I let him get ahead and then stooped and picked up my paper sack, trying to make it look casual. When I straightened I found the twinkling eyes of the old man watching me.

He nodded as I went out the door, following Rose who was halfway across the street. The twinkle in his eyes had faded. He looked sad. I wanted to tell him not to waste any sadness over me, but I didn't want to hurt his feelings, so I let it go.

Rose was behind the lobby desk when I got in there.

"Can you start at eight-thirty tonight?" he said.

"On the nose," I said.

"Got a dinner jacket?"

"No."

"I'll talk to the waiters. Maybe we can find one. You better get a black tie and white front."

"Sure," I said. "The room will be ready at five?"

"Not later than that," he said. "It's off the service entrance around the back. You can come in through here, if you want to."

"Thanks."

I walked out of the lobby into the street, carrying the bottle. Sunlight lay on the sidewalks and on the fronts of the stores like baked enamel. The air was dry and had the smell of dust and chaff in it. The street was busy and crowded with women shopping. At least half of them pushed baby carriages. On benches here and there along the street sat old men, smoking and chewing and watching the traffic go by.

I walked south down the street toward the end of town where I'd left Connie. I had been gone longer than half an hour, but I figured on its taking her a while to pick out what she wanted and could pay for.

When I got to the variety store where we'd parted, she wasn't anywhere in sight. I looked inside and she wasn't in there either. I looked around the corner of the store into an alley that ran back beside it and she wasn't there. She was nowhere in sight on the street that I could see.

I felt sudden fear, and then was ashamed of it. I switched to a feeling of relief that she was off my hands, and felt even more shame. I walked back into the alley beside the store, pushed the open end of the sack down out of the way, took the cap off the bottle and had a long drink. I wanted another one, but I forced myself to replace the cap and cover the bottle. I looked around for a place to hide it and found a couple of likely spots, but I was afraid to try it. You never know who's watching. Then there are people who can smell whisky a block away. I carried it with me back to the sidewalk.

Then I saw her, far down toward the end of town, walking away toward the railroad tracks. The clothes were different and there were shoes on her feet, but there was no mistake about her tiny figure, the long dark hair, the shy, dogged stride, like that of a wounded animal.

For a moment I felt a bitter charge of resentment that she hadn't waited. But it passed and I got a firm grip on the bottle and went after her, walking fast along the sun-baked street.

She had almost reached the tracks when I caught up with her. She heard the steps behind her, took one quick, panic-stricken look over her shoulder and started to run. Then it registered with her who I was and she stopped and let me walk up to her.

She wore a plain white dress with puff sleeves and a tight bodice. The skirt was gathered around her waist and flared out below. She wore white ankle socks and gray ballet slippers. She had gathered her hair together in back and tied a white ribbon around it. Under her arm she carried the old slicker and I guessed that inside were her old dress and probably the remains of the sandwich she'd chewed at while we were on the train.

Her eyes were dull as she looked at me, but fear lurked in their corners.

"Where were you going?" I asked.

She looked down.

"I thought you weren't coming. I waited."

"You were going to catch another freight."

"Yes."

"In that outfit?"

"Yes."

She looked down at her skirt.

"Excuse me," I said. "You look real cute."

She dug around in the slicker and when her hand came back out there were three dollar bills in it wrapped around some small change. She held it out to me.

"It only cost sixteen dollars and forty-three cents," she said. "Here's the change."

"I don't need it," I said. "I got a job."

"A job? Doing what?"

"I'm a piano player," I said. "You must be hungry."

"Yes."

"Let's find a place to eat."

"I have to keep going," she said. "I have to get back home."

"We'll talk about that," I said.

I took her arm and she came along with me back toward town. We stopped at a placed called Ernie's Café. It looked like our style. Plenty of food for not much money.

She ate like a starved dog. She didn't talk or look up or pay any attention to anything that went on in the place. She just sat with her eyes on her plate and put away the food—eggs, bacon, toast, a stack of hot cakes, fried potatoes, coffee and milk. My own appetite was skimpy, as usual. Connie finished up what I left. When she finally sat back in her chair I asked whether she wanted more and she shook her head.

"Didn't they ever feed you?" I said.

"Most of the time," she said. "Except when they got mad at me."

"Why would they get mad?"

She looked away and didn't answer.

"Look," I said. "If you're Connie Jordan, your sister and her attorneys, or whoever handles things, would probably be glad to hear from you."

Her eyes came to life for a moment.

"Yes," she said.

"They'd probably send you money so you could fly home, or take the train—inside. They might even send somebody to pick you up."

"How would they know it was really me?" she said.

"I was thinking, if you'd call your sister on the phone—" Her eyes were fully alive now. They grabbed mine and held. She leaned across the table.

"Could I?" she said.

"Sure. Your sister's got millions of bucks. Why should you ride home in a boxcar? Or even on a bus? She'll probably be so glad to hear from you, she'll come out personally to see you get home all right."

Her face was like the night before Christmas.

"Jeanie," she said softly. "I'll see Jeanie again."

Then she looked hopeless again for a minute.

"But I'll never see my father."

"Who knows?" I said.

She came alive again and leaned toward me.

"How soon can I call her?"

"Seven o'clock," I said.

"Will you stay with me? And show me how?"

"Didn't you ever call long distance on the telephone?" She looked a little ashamed.

"I haven't called anybody on the phone for eight years."

"I'll stay with you," I said.

I looked around the little restaurant. There were three or four customers seated at the linoleum-topped counter along one side. The proprietor was a heavy-set, black-haired guy with muscular, tattooed arms and a big bush of black hair sticking out of his shirt below his neck.

"Excuse me," I said to Connie and got up and went back to the end of the counter where I had seen a telephone.

The proprietor came back to see what I wanted. I gave him a dime.

"Can I use the phone?" I said.

"Sure. Go ahead," he said.

"I want to call the local law," I said.

"Constable or sheriff?" he said.

"Better make it the sheriff."

"Just ask the operator. We only got a deputy office here. Sam Freed's the deputy. If he's in."

"Thanks," I said.

I lifted the phone and asked the operator for the sheriff's office.

"I'll try it," she said.

I waited and she rang, letting it ring a long time. Finally she came back on the line and said, "He doesn't seem to be in the office. I'll try him at home. Is it an emergency?"

"It could be," I said.

"Just a moment," she said.

I waited some more and pretty soon there was a click at the other end and a woman answered. Before I could say anything the operator said, "Hello, Mrs. Freed. I have a call here for Sam."

"I'll call him," the woman said.

Finally a man's voice came on. He sounded sleepy. "Hello," I said, "do you remember the Jordan case?"

There was a pause, then he said, "Can't say I do."

"A kidnapping in California," I said. "Eight years old."

"Wait a minute."

I waited while he thought about it.

"Young girl with a rich father?" he said. "They never found her?"

"That's the one. Connie Jordan was her name."

"Yeah. I remember now."

I took a deep breath.

"Well, what would you say if I told you that the Jordan girl is with me, right here in town?"

There was a long pause. Then he said, "I'd say you were nuts."

"That's what I thought you'd say, but tell me why?"

"All right," he said. "Number one: the Jordan girl was declared dead by a Los Angeles court about a year ago. I read that in a paper."

"So did I," I said. "But that's just a legal terminology."

"I know it," he said. "But there's something else. Number two."

"Let me have it," I said.

"About six months ago I got a bulletin in here. Said the remains of the Jordan girl had been found in a shallow grave in the desert near San Ber—let's see—"

"San Bernardino?" I said.

"That's it. The remains were positively identified as those of the Jordan girl."

"How can they be sure."

"I don't know. But that's what the bulletin said. We had a flock of 'em at the time of her kidnapping. F.B.I. was looking all over for her."

"But they're not looking anymore?"

"I guess not. Who are you, stranger?"

"It doesn't matter," I said. "Thanks."

I hung up.

CHAPTER 6

On the way back to the table I thought it over. So she was a fake. Or she was a ghost. Or she was real and the remains they'd dug up near San Bernardino were somebody else's. Or I had left off being sane. And when she called her sister, later in the day, what would they say to each other—a dead girl and the heiress to a major fortune?

And how had I let myself get mixed up in it? I, who wanted everything simple and uncomplicated and no problems, no decisions?

I sat down across from her and I couldn't look at her, because I couldn't think of anything to say. She waited for me to say something and finally I reached down to where I'd set the bottle on the floor near a leg of the table, glanced around to see whether the proprietor was looking, got the cap off and poured a generous shot into my water glass. I drank it slowly, avoiding her eyes. But I felt her staring at the glass.

"So I drink," I said.

"I didn't say anything," she said.

"Well, don't," I said.

She kept quiet then and I drank the lukewarm highball slowly, trying to think, knowing I wasn't really thinking, but only thrashing around in my mind, trying to find a way out. When she spoke, I was startled and nearly jumped out of my chair.

"What are we going to do?" she said.

"I don't know," I said. "I guess maybe we could go window-shopping."

"All right," she said and stood up.

I settled the bill with the hairy-chested proprietor and we stepped out into the sunlight. We stood there for a minute, looking both ways.

"What was his name?" I asked, "the one I hit with the rock?"

"Kretch," she said.

I repeated it.

"And the woman's name was Madeline and there was a girl named Mitzi."

"Yes," she said.

"What did they do?"

"What do you mean?"

"With the carnival. What kind of thing did they have with the carnival?"

She hesitated, as she always did when we got on that subject.

"They called it a—'girlie' show."

"I see. And you were one of the 'girlies'."

It was brutal the way I said it and I hadn't meant it to be brutal. She shrank away from me and I reached out and put my arm around her waist. She was stiff and tight like a wound-up spring.

"Sorry," I said. "Don't pay any attention to me. I'm a lush and things get kind of complicated."

She didn't loosen up any.

"What's a lush?"

"A guy that drinks more than he eats," I said.

She stood there, stiff and tight, staring at me, and finally she said, "I'm sorry I made trouble for you."

"I'm sorry too," I said. "But we'd better stick together for a while longer."

She relaxed a little then, not completely.

"What's the matter?" I said.

"Kretch. I'm afraid—"

"The hell with him," I said. "He doesn't know where we are."

"He'll find out. He'll come and get me."

I put my hands on her arms and turned her so I could look into her face. It was drawn and tight and frightened. Her eyes had that flat look again.

"Listen," I said, "I don't know how I came to get mixed up in this, but I'm in it—with you. I think there's a good chance you'll make it back to Los Angeles. But you'll never make it if you don't relax and think ahead instead of back. Because you'll die before you get there. You'll scare yourself to death."

She flared up for a moment. It was the first time.

"You'd be scared too!" she said.

I grinned at her.

"Good," I said. "Now you're showing some fight. Just string along, kid, and we'll make out fine."

A smile twisted the corners of her mouth, but it didn't last.

"I've got a room reserved for us," I told her, "in the best hotel in town. But it won't be ready till five o'clock. Let's find a place where we can sit down and keep cool from now till then."

We went on along the main street, past the hotel, beyond the business section, and the street widened. We turned at a corner and ahead of us was a small park, with children's playground equipment here and there.

We sat down on the grass under a tree. Connie stretched out and fell asleep. I took a couple of drinks from my bottle. I wanted to attain that rare state known as the "rosy glow." It wasn't easy to reach and it was even harder to maintain it. My usual habit was to get dead drunk. But now I didn't dare get drunk before I'd done something about Connie. I had tried to walk away from her but found I couldn't. It scared me to think that if I got drunk enough I might not care anymore. I might find I could walk away from her. I was afraid to find that out about myself.

I had enough to know about myself without taking on anything new. I sat there with my fingers clasped stiffly around the bottle, trying to keep it from coming back.

But it came—the dingy swirl of memories, the endless, grinding hours of practice, hating it, with my mother cracking the whip…the day I woke, half-man, half-boy, to realize my father had gone away, would never be back…the awful homesickness East at the conservatory, the cruel competition; running away and getting scared, sneaking back with the shame of it under my ribs…the finishing in spite of all, the diploma, and them saying, "Now you must give a recital"—the plans for it, twelve hours a day polishing the repertoire—the big time—the bright hope… and then suddenly no money—no sponsor—no hall—no recital…twenty years old and a handful of talent…and a one-way bus ticket back to California.

What did you do? You went to work—a big commercial band. Touring. Always plenty to drink and plenty of money to buy it. You never liked it, but you liked the effect—when you remembered your father, or the recital that never came off, when you were lonely, as you always were—the effect was wonderful… Wonderful like the little blonde doll in Cleveland. Every night for a week she stood there beside the keyboard, eyes closed, lips parted, from the time the hall opened till the boys began packing their instruments, and the first time you spoke to her, yours was the voice of God. A set-up the boys said, a pigeon. Don't be so shy, kid!

A wild, beautiful week and at the end of it you and the little blonde were married. You twenty-one, she eighteen. The boys shrugged. Maybe not quite such a set-up after all. She held out for a ring… So it goes. Have another drink…

The bottle and I managed to block it out finally. I looked down at Connie, asleep on the grass. I looked at her for a long time and then I took one more long pull from the bottle and after a while I woke her up.

Waking, she was startled and scared, as usual, but then she recognized me and quieted down. I said it was time to go to the hotel.

"How did you get the room?" she asked.

"It's part of my pay." I looked away from her. "I told them you were my wife."

When I turned back, she was looking at me out of those brown eyes.

The room, with its brass bed and worn bureau, dressing table with mirror and one overstuffed chair, was small and dark, but clean. It had a shower but no tub. It opened off a corridor that ran the length of the hotel from front to back. We were twenty feet along the hall from the rear service entrance, a steel door with iron bars over a frosted glass panel. Farther along toward the front was the service entrance to the Zephyr Room and opposite that a back stairway led to the hotel kitchen.

Connie sat on the edge of the bed and ran her hand over the clean, white spread. Her eyes traveled slowly about the room, lingering over every piece of furniture. She pulled back the spread and ran her hand over the clean pillow slip.

"Didn't they give you a bed sheet either?" I said.

She shook her head.

"I slept on a straw mattress in the tent. Sometimes in the car."

Her eyes slipped toward the open door of the bathroom.

"A shower bath," she said softly.

"Sure. Soap and towels on the house," I said.

She took off her shoes and ankle socks. She started to pull the new dress off, then stopped and looked at me over her shoulder.

"I'll go out for a while," I said, turning to the door.

By the time I reached it her voice came quietly across the room.

"Chris—" I turned back. "You don't have to go if you don't want to. It's like we were married. It feels like that."

I felt laughter inside, a grim kind of laughter.

"If it's a good feeling, kid," I said, "then all right. I've been married before."

After a while she said, "Oh."

Mentioning it had brought it back. I picked up my bottle, found a glass in the bathroom and poured a generous shot. I drank it fast, chasing it with some water. Connie had undressed. I glanced at her and glanced away. She went into the bathroom and closed the door and pretty soon I heard the water running in the shower.

It took me back again, in spite of everything I could do to block the memory...

The "wonderful" little blonde from Cleveland—O.K. as a hepcat, following the band, sitting devotedly by the piano, full of sweet passion while the beat of the music lingered in her head... But as a wife, later, after the tour and the job had ended and no new job for weeks, sitting around in the cheap Hollywood apartment with nothing to do, nothing to think about—how then?

Not so good. And the price of the wild, wonderful nights on the road? A normal price, a baby coming, a good, normal thing. Only she didn't want it—tried everything, nothing worked—stormed and raved against it and more and more drinking, because it took a little more each time to drown the desperation—for both of us.

Then another job on the road and more screaming because she couldn't go too, but we needed the money... And the homecoming—the baby here now, a boy, cute but sickly. But she didn't care. And the price of not caring? The price of neglect, of frustration, of endless, hateful bickering? The baby paid it with a life that never really got started—the doctor puzzled and cold: "Sometimes if they're not wanted, they just take the quick way out. Maybe they're lucky."

And then the marriage going down. God, how they go down! Like ships on a reef, foundering in a crazy welter of sound and fury, smashed glass and a thin trickle of whisky running across the floor...

The shower water stopped suddenly, jerking me out of the daydream. My fingers clutched convulsively at the bottle's neck and I turned slowly to look at the closed bathroom door.

Have I done it again? I thought. Have I picked up a girl on impulse, without thinking or caring, who will turn out like the other one? Will it happen all over again the same way?

There was no way for me to bridge the gap between the kidnapped daughter of a multimillionaire and the bedraggled, skinny girl who had come out of the river by the railroad tracks. It was too big a jump. I couldn't go for it. But I didn't have any more proof than she did.

The newspaper story had said the Jordan girl had markings on her body that would identify her. I couldn't know what the marks were supposed to be like. If this girl with me had figured on faking some marks, maybe right now would be the time to check on it. It would be hard for her to hide anything, fresh out of the shower.

But that pondering didn't mean a thing. Whoever she was, she was here with me and I was stuck with her. I was almost as sorry for her as I was for myself. She'd picked the last man who could do her any good.

Maybe I could make enough in the kitty to buy her a bus ticket to Los Angeles. That would get her off my hands and take care of my conscience at the same time. I wondered how many days and how much alcohol it would take to drown that goddam conscience. I'd worked at it pretty steadily now for five years.

I weaved over to the bed and lay down. I closed my eyes and told myself it was a dream. It was all just something I'd dreamed up, a nightmare, and none of it had really happened. The bathroom door would never open. She'd never come out.

But the bathroom door did open. The girl did come out. She held a towel up in front of her and she walked toward the bed slowly, uncertainly. I blinked at her, but she didn't go away. She came to the edge of the bed and stood there, looking down at me with wide, brown eyes. She had washed her hair and it hung damply around her face and over her bare shoulders. She smelled of soap and dampness.

"So you are Connie Jordan," I said out of my private fog.

"Yes, Chris."

"The thing in the paper—it said there were marks on your body—identification—" She looked at me for a while and then she nodded.

"Do you want to see them?" she said.

"Why not?"

She stood for a while, as if thinking it over. Anybody could have marks on her body. How would I know whether the marks on this girl were the same as those on Connie Jordan? She must have been thinking about that.

She was holding the towel just above her breasts with her left arm. I noticed she had taken off the ring.

"For one place," she said slowly, "in my mouth. I wore braces till I was twelve. They used to hurt. They made marks too. The dentist could tell."

"O.K.," I said. "Where else?"

She hesitated a moment, then lowered her left arm, so that the towel folded down on her waist. She put her hand on her left breast and raised it slightly. Just below it, dark against her pale skin, were three small moles, forming a triangle maybe half an inch on each side.

"These," she said.

"Yeah," I said. "Any more?"

She made a half-turn, standing with her left hip toward me, her shoulders twisted away. High on her hip was a small pink birthmark, a kind of rosette about an inch in diameter.

I felt a little silly. She'd shown me the marks, but I didn't know any more than I had before. How could I know whether they were the right marks?

I sat up on the bed and began to take off my shoes and socks.

"All right," I said. "Maybe you could get some more sleep while I take a shower."

I couldn't look at her. I heard her crawling into bed behind me. The springs squeaked on the old brass bed. When I got my clothes off I glanced around. She lay on the far side of the bed, covered to the chin, her head turned away so that she faced the wall. I headed for the shower.

"Chris—" she said.

"Yeah?"

"Do you believe me now—that I'm Connie Jordan?"

I thought about it.

"I won't say I don't," I said. "But it's a long jump. We'll see what happens."

She didn't answer. I went on into the bathroom and closed the door.

The shower washed away some of my tension. I began to think maybe I was worrying too much. Maybe I ought to relax and take advantage of what was right here in front of me.

When I came out of the shower, Connie was crowded over against the far wall, staring at me, with that look of fear in her face that I'd seen before.

"Look, kid," I said, "we're practically man and wife."

"Chris—" I tried to pull the bedclothes down, but she held onto them tightly. I jerked at them again and she lost her grip. I put my hand on her breast and felt her shivering.

"No, Chris!" she said. "Please—no!"

"You were willing this morning," I said.

Suddenly she was fighting me. She came at me with her fingernails, clawing and scratching. I caught her hands, forcing her back down on the bed. She looked straight into my eyes and spat in my face.

I let go of her, crawled off the bed and went in the bathroom. When I came back I stood and looked at her. She was crying. Large drops welled out of her eyes, ran down her pale, thin cheeks.

"Well, all right," I said. "Please forgive me."

I made quite a production out of it. I grabbed the pillow on my side of the bed, threw it on the floor and stretched out with my head on it. I drank two or three shots from my bottle. I lay there for a long time, feeling the rug scratching me, feeling self-righteous. And then, after a long time, Connie began to talk. Her voice from where she lay on the bed seemed to come from a distance.

"They picked me up on the street after school," she said. "I was on my way home. They stopped and asked me how to get someplace. And when I went over to the car, they—grabbed me and held me and put me inside. Kretch sat in the back seat and held me down on the floor.

"For a long time I kept knowing my father would come and save me. But he never did. And after a while I gave up. I cried at lot at first, but then I couldn't cry any more. I just did whatever they told me. Sometimes, even when I did what they wanted, they'd get angry and Kretch would hit me. Madeleine hit me sometimes too, but most of the time she didn't pay any attention.

"We would go to hotels. If they had to go out they would make me take some pills that put me to sleep. There was never a telephone in the room. But they hardly ever left me alone. Mostly I slept. Even when I wasn't sleeping, I felt sleepy."

The bedsprings squeaked lightly. I lay still on the floor, waiting for her to go on, half-wishing she wouldn't.

"One day—" her voice was fainter now, farther away—"Madeleine went out and left me with Kretch. I was on one of the beds and I went to sleep. I woke up and he was coming—out of the bathroom. He was—undressed. He came over to the bed and told me to take off my clothes. I was scared and said I wouldn't. He pushed my dress up and I began to fight him. Then he hit me. He hit me hard—so many times—and I fainted and didn't know any more.

"When I woke up I hurt very badly and I was bleeding. I was afraid to look at myself. Madeleine was there and she was cursing at Kretch and hitting him with her purse. Kretch just sat and let her hit him until she got tired of it. Then she came over and did something to me, I don't know what, but pretty soon it didn't hurt so much and I went back to sleep. We stayed in that place for three days, because it hurt me to walk."

She paused again.

"Look, Connie," I said, "you don't have to—"

"Then we drove way out in the country to a place where there were tents and things—a carnival. There was a girl there waiting for us. Her name was Mitzi. Mitzi and Madeleine were in the show. Madeleine was big and ugly, but she wasn't fat. There was a big tent with a stage in it where they had the show and then there was another, smaller tent in back. Kretch stood out in front and sold the tickets till the show started. Then he would come back to the little tent and stay with me. He never talked to me. He would just sit there and wait till the show was over and Madeleine came back to the tent.

"Mitzi said they didn't make me be in the show because I was a minor. They were afraid the police might not like it. So they never let anybody see me in the daytime. I tried to tell Mitzi who I was, when I could be alone with her, but she wouldn't believe me. She told me even if it was true, there was nothing she could do about it. She was the only one who ever said anything nice to me. At first I didn't know anything about the show and then Mitzi told me that they just danced a little and when there weren't any policemen, sometimes they would take off all their clothes.

"There were trucks that carried the big tents when we moved to a new place. Kretch and Madeleine had a trailer and Mitzi would stay in the trailer, while Kretch and Madeleine drove the car. I would sleep in the back seat of the car. But when we stopped anywhere for a show, I had to sleep in the little tent. Sometimes Madeleine would sleep with me and sometimes Kretch—but he never tried to do anything to me again. Sometimes they would give me some of the pills so I would be sure to sleep."

"You never had a chance to get away?"

"No. If they had to leave me alone for a little while, they would tie me up, or else give me the pills so I would sleep."

"And you didn't do anything all that time—except ride in the car and sleep?"

"At first. And then one night after the show Madeleine came in the little tent and said it was time I began to pay my own way. She said she was going to bring a man to the tent. When I asked her what for she just said if I didn't know what to do, the man would show me. She made me pull my dress up. I was afraid of her and I didn't fight her. I was afraid of the man, too, but I was more afraid of Madeleine. I was afraid all the time. But the man didn't hurt me as much as Kretch did—that first time."

I lay on the floor and looked at the ceiling. The floor was cold under me, but I was cold on the inside too.

"After that," Connie said, "there were a lot of men. Sometimes a man would come in and look at me and get angry. I would hear him tell Madeleine, 'She's only a kid, goddam it.' Then we would pack up everything and leave that place."

My voice felt rough in my throat.

"When did you find the newspaper clipping?" I said.

"Kretch had the paper in the car. When he got through with it he put in on the floor in the back and when I was alone I started to read it. I found that story about my father—and about me—and I tore it out and hid it. It made me feel better. I thought maybe someday I might be able to get away. And it made me feel closer to Jeanie—my sister—just to have the story."

There was a long silence. Finally I broke it.

"How did you get away?"

"I was in the tent. It was near the river. The show had just started, and Kretch hadn't come back yet. They hadn't tied me up. I had two sandwiches they'd brought me for supper and I wrapped them up in the slicker. There was a lot of noise out in front and I could hear Kretch and Madeleine in the big tent, arguing. I went out of the tent and sneaked behind the trailer toward the trees and the river. Mitzi came out of the trailer and stopped when she saw me. I told her I was going to run away.

She didn't try to stop me. She just said, 'Good luck, kid,' and I started to run.

"I'd seen the trains going by on the other side of the river and I thought if I could get across there I might be able to get on a train and if I would tell somebody who I was, they would help me. But I couldn't swim. I waded into the river and it got up to my neck and then it carried me away. I almost drowned. All I could do was kick my feet and hold onto the slicker and try to keep my head up. And after a long time I felt the bottom again and I walked out. And when I saw you—and you picked up that rock…"

The room was very dark now. I began to shiver from the cold. I got up and found my way to the bottle and took a long, drink. I groped around and found my clothes and put them on.

"It must be seven o'clock," I said. "We'd better put in that call to your sister, Jeanie."

The bedsprings squeaked. I sat down in the armchair in the dark and waited for her to dress.

CHAPTER 7

The Zephyr Room was cool, dimly lighted and quiet. There were no customers. A bartender was getting set for the evening, dusting bottles and ash trays. The old upright piano sat on the platform in the corner. It looked like home.

Connie and I sat down at the bar and the bartender walked our way. He was short and wide in the shoulders and his nose had been broken once so that it was flattened and pushed to one side.

"I'm the piano player," I said.

He nodded.

"Art told me."

"This is my wife, Connie."

He held out his hand.

"I'm Joe Burns."

Connie took his hand shyly.

"We need something to eat and to make a phone call," I said.

He pointed to the far end of the bar.

"There's a public phone on the wall," he said. "If you want to eat in here, I'll have a girl come down and tell you what we've got."

"Real great," I said. "How are you fixed for change?"

He nodded and I handed him three dollar bills. He opened the cash register and came back with a handful of quarters, dimes and nickels. I poured them into Connie's two hands and led her to the end of the bar. She stood there, looking first at the telephone, then at me, then at the change in her hands.

"Will you do it for me?" she whispered.

She held out the money.

"All right. It may take a while to get a line," I said.

There was no dial. I lifted the receiver and got an operator.

"I want to place a person-to-person call to Jean Jordan," I said. "She lives in West Los Angeles, California."

"Do you know the number?" she asked.

I glanced at Connie.

"Do you remember your telephone number?"

She shook her head. Her eyes were pleading with me.

"Address?" I said.

She thought about it, shook her head again.

"All I know," I told the operator, "is the name Jean Jordan and she lives in West Los Angeles."

"I'll try," the operator said.

I listened while she tried to get a line. After a while she said, "I'm sorry, but the circuits are busy. I'll call you back. Your number, please?"

I gave her the number and hung up.

"We'll have to wait a while," I said to Connie.

Her eyes had never left my face. I could feel them burning into mine.

"Do you think I'll get a chance to talk to her?"

"Sure. Try not to worry."

A waitress came in and Connie and I sat down at one of the cocktail tables lined up along the wall between the piano and the telephone. I ordered a dinner for Connie and a corned beef on rye for myself with a bottle of beer. The bartender came over with the beer.

"Thanks, Joe," I said. "There's something you ought to know."

"Yeah?"

"I haven't got around yet to joining the AA. Especially when I'm working. I mentioned it to Mr. Rose."

Joe was all right. He grinned.

"I'll try to keep you from running dry," he said. "I've got a percentage to watch, though."

"We'll work something out," I said.

"O.K."

He went away.

Connie was twisting her hands on the table top. I put one of mine over them.

"Everything will work out," I said.

The waitress brought the food. It was good food and I ate all my sandwich. Connie didn't eat much. She pushed the stuff around on the plate and stared into space.

"Try to eat," I said. "You need more meat on your bones."

"I'm not hungry. I wish I could talk to Jeanie."

"Pretty soon," I said. And then I said, "Connie—it might be—it's been a long time—she might not recognize your voice."

"I know—"

"There've been a lot of girls who claimed to be you. She might not believe it."

"But after I talk to her—"

"Sure. But I don't want you to be disappointed—"

I couldn't bring myself to tell her what the sheriff's deputy had told me—that the remains of Connie Jordan had been found near San Bernardino. I tried to start her thinking about something else.

"I don't want you to go back to the room," I said. "I want you in here where I can see you. Besides I need some help."

"All right, Chris."

"I'll put a kitty on top of the piano. That's for people to put money in, if they like what I play. I'm going to give you a couple of dollars and after I've been playing for a while, I want you to get up and come to the piano and put one of the bills in the kitty."

She stared at me.

"But it's your own money."

"I know. But it will give people the idea. Maybe get them started. The only way I have to make any cash money is to get it in the kitty."

"Is it really a kitty?"

I laughed.

"No. It's just an empty highball glass. They call it a kitty."

"Can you really play the piano?"

"I'll give you a demonstration," I said. "It's time to warm up anyway."

I went to the upright and ran my fingers up and down the keyboard lightly. My fingers were stiff. The instrument had a stiff action and the combination was stiffer than I'd wanted. But I could make out. Besides, I had some time to practice. There were still no customers in the place and Joe, the bartender, and Connie were the whole audience.

I improvised for a while on some standard themes and little by little I loosened up. My facility had been shot some time before and I didn't hit all the notes I planned to, but I could get by. My mind wasn't as foggy as it would get later and I could still hear fairly well.

The hell with it, I thought. You don't have to be a genius. All you have to do is get that kitty filled up every night for a week. Get enough to buy a bus ticket to Los Angeles. Maybe two bus tickets.

The piano was set at an angle that made most of the room visible to me. I could look over my right shoulder along the wall where Connie sat at a table and to the bar at the other end of the room.

Art Rose came in through the service door and handed a package to Joe. He stayed a while, watching me, but I couldn't tell whether he was listening. I nodded at him but he didn't nod back. After a while he left. Joe came to the piano and handed me a white jacket.

"Art told me you'd wear this," he said.

I tried it on, while Joe waited. The sleeves were a little short, but it would do.

"You're pretty good on that thing," Joe said.

"I'm not Art Tatum," I said. Then: "I'm partial to bourbon and water."

"Who isn't?" he said.

"No hurry," I said.

He grinned and walked away toward the bar. I glanced at Connie. She sat stiff and straight with her back against the wall. Joe brought me a drink and I carried it back to the table. Connie didn't say anything. I don't think any girl in the world ever waited so hard for a phone call.

I had picked up an empty glass at the bar. I showed it to Connie and handed her a couple of bills.

"This is the kitty," I said. "I'll let you know when to put the money in."

"All right, Chris," she said.

I set the glass on top of the piano. The telephone rang. The bell was loud and shrill in the small room. I froze, looking at Connie. She leaned forward over the table and was staring at the telephone on the wall. It rang again and I started toward it. It rang once more before I got there, Connie trailing along behind.

"On your call to Los Angeles," the operator said, "there is no listing for a Jean Jordan."

"It may be unlisted," I said. "It's very important—" Connie was leaning against the wall beside the phone, staring at me.

"I'm sorry, sir," the operator said.

"Wait! Don't break the connection. I'm placing this call for Jean Jordan's sister—Connie." I hoped the Los Angeles operator would hear me and remember. "Connie Jordan was kidnapped—"

"I'm sorry, sir, but information can't give me that—"

The Los Angeles operator broke in. I heard her say, "Hello, operator. I'll try to complete the call. I'll call you back."

"Thank you," said the local girl.

There was sweat on my forehead when I hung up. I patted Connie's shoulder.

"Little while longer," I said. "Would you like a drink?" She sat down at the table.

"Would it taste like the one you gave me on the train?" she said.

"Doesn't have to taste like that."

"I'll try it," she said. "Pick it out for me, Chris."

I asked Joe to make her a brandy Alexander. Connie tasted it and nodded a thank you. There were tears in her eyes and I couldn't think of much to say. It was almost time for me to go to work. Two men had come in and sat down at the bar. I waited till Joe got through with them before asking him to fix up my highball. He made a good one and I picked it up and headed back toward the piano. I gave Connie a forced smile as I passed her and she was still crying. But I had already begun to think about the keyboard.

I was half a dozen bars into "Melancholy Baby" when the telephone rang again. I glanced at Connie. She was leaning forward, the same as before, and, as before, she was frozen. I flashed her a signal with the flat of my hand, meaning she should hold on, and let Joe take the call. I watched him answer and after a moment he lowered the receiver and motioned to me. I got down and started toward the phone, helping Connie up as I passed the table. Again she came along and leaned against the wall beside me.

"I have Miss Jean Jordan in Los Angeles," the operator said. "Deposit two-twenty-five, please, for three minutes."

I fed nine quarters into the slot. They clanged and banged going down.

"Hello," I said.

There was a pause and a woman's voice said, "Hello—this is Jean Jordan."

Her voice, picked up, amplified, boosted and amplified again across the twenty-five hundred miles between us, sounded dry and mechanical.

"Just a minute," I said. "I have your sister, Connie."

There was another pause and she said, "My sister is dead."

"Please hold on just a minute," I said.

I handed the receiver to Connie and pushed her in front of the phone. She had to stand on tiptoe to reach the mouthpiece. She looked at me, scared to death, and I said, "Say hello and then just keep talking."

"Hello," she said.

There was a long silence. Too long. I was afraid the girl on the other end might hang up.

"This is Connie," I whispered in her ear and she repeated it. Finally she got with it.

"But, Jeanie—" she said. "Don't you remember?... I'm Connie. I got away—" I couldn't stand it any longer. I walked back along the bar and leaned on it. I heard snatches of phrases: (...but I'm alive, Jeanie!... Westbrook, Indiana...but, Jeanie—...all right...all right, Jeanie..."

I heard the receiver click. I walked back to the piano and started to play. At first I couldn't hear what I was playing—only Connie's voice and the sound of the quarters dropping into the box. I looked that way finally and Connie was coming toward me, walking as if asleep, with her hands out in front of her. One of the men at the bar had turned and was watching her. I waited for her to make the trip.

She climbed up on the platform and held onto the piano, staring at me.

"Chris—she said I was dead. She didn't believe me—"

"It's been a long time, honey."

"But she didn't even listen. She said to go to the F.B.I."

"Then that's what we'll do," I said.

"How can we? Where do we have to go?"

"They'll have an office somewhere close. Try not to think about it. Try to listen to the music."

"Chris—" I finished the piece and laid a hand over one of hers.

"Please, Connie, I have to keep working, or we won't be able to go anywhere. Just sit down and try to think of something else. Pretty soon you can come and put a dollar in the kitty."

"All right, Chris."

She walked away toward the cocktail table. I went to work on "Begin and Beguine," playing it loud and fast. I missed a lot of notes, but I made plenty of noise. The guys at the bar watched me for a while, then turned back to talk to Joe. That was all right with me.

Business was spotty and slow. By ten-thirty there were half a dozen people at tables here and there on the floor, and four or five men at the bar. Nobody had paid any attention to the music as far as I could tell. I finished a set with a watered-down arrangement of "Tea for Two," sacrificing accuracy for tempo, and when I'd finished I nodded to Connie and she came up and put a dollar bill in the kitty. Nobody rushed to follow suit. I took a break.

Between eleven and one A.M., when the place closed, there was considerable business and I made a few dollars. Precisely, I made four dollars and forty-eight cents. I don't know where the pennies came from, but I didn't throw them out. At this rate, it would take a long time to earn a bus ticket. But maybe the people who'd liked me would come back and bring their friends.

I had a quick one at the bar after we closed and when I went to the table to get Connie, she was sound asleep with her head against the wall. I picked her up and carried her to our room and by then she had waked up enough to walk to the bed.

"What will we do now, Chris?" she said.

"In the morning," I said, "we'll go see the sheriff and contact the F.B.I."

She went to sleep. My nerves were on fire and I lay there and sucked on my bottle till I passed out. It always worked. It had never failed me yet.

The sheriff's deputy, Sam Freed, was tall, gangly and poker-faced. He was missing a finger on his left hand and there was a crease over his right eye that might have been made by a bullet, or opened up with a blunt instrument. He had a little office adjoining his house, and he sat in a swivel chair with his eyes closed while I told him all I knew about Connie, starting at the time the freight train stopped across the river from the carnival.

When I finished, he looked at me for a long time, then he pushed his chair around and looked at Connie. There was no expression on his face. Pretty soon he picked up a telephone and asked the operator to get him the sheriff's office in the county seat. When he got the man he wanted, he spoke into the phone:

"Sam Freed talkin'. There's a carnival operatin' over southeast—maybe the other side of Columbus—maybe followin' the B. & O. line. Might be the F.B.I. would want to check up on a couple down there—woman named Madeleine and a man named—" He glanced at Connie.

"Kretch," she said.

"Kretch," Freed said to the phone. "Also a girl with them named Mitzi. A girlie show…yeah… There was another girl too, but she's in my office right now. Claims to be the missing Jordan girl… Jordan… kidnapped a number of years ago in California… That's right… Can you give me a line to the F.B.I.?"

He hung on for a while and pretty soon he was talking again.

(…could you send somebody down here to check on this girl?… I don't know, but the story's good. The age looks right… Yeah, I'll hold on."

He looked at Connie again and ran his hand over his face. He looked a little embarrassed.

"Says to ask you if you got three moles under your breast."

Connie nodded quickly.

"Which one?" Freed asked.

"The left one."

He repeated this into the phone and listened and then he said, "Around nine o'clock? All right. I'll see she's here."

He hung up and looked at me.

"This agent will come over. Be tonight some time. Where you stayin'?"

I told him.

"Workin' in town, are you?" he said.

"For Art Rose."

He kept looking at me.

"What kind of work you doin'?"

"I'm a piano player."

His fingers began playing with a clutter of papers on the desk, but his eyes stayed on me.

"Just get started, did you?" he said.

"Last night."

I stood up. I didn't like the questions.

"We better go," I said.

He stood up, too, and nodded shortly.

"That's all I can do right now," he said. "I'll call you when the F.B.I. agent gets here."

"Thanks," I said.

He watched us go out. He was watching when I glanced back from the door. His face was still impassive.

Connie was wound up tight again. I lay on the bed in the hotel room, holding my bottle in one hand, watching her pace the floor. After a while we went upstairs to the coffee shop and had lunch. When we finished it was one-thirty in the afternoon—a long, long time before nine in the evening.

We walked down the street and found a theater that opened at two o'clock. We hung around till it opened and went inside. When we got out on the street again it was five-thirty. I reached for her hand and she gripped mine tightly. Hers was damp.

Back in the room, Connie wanted to take a bath. This time, I didn't hang around. I told her I was going into the Zephyr Room to practice and I didn't go to the room again till after she had bathed and dressed and come out to find me.

I went to work at eight o'clock and Connie sat at the cocktail table with her head against the wall, twisting her fingers endlessly, staring straight ahead. My own fingers were practically useless. If it was going to go on like this for days, I'd have to quit. It took more and more liquor to break down my tension and Joe wasn't as friendly as he had been the night before. Business was better, though. Three gay couples came in and put some money in the kitty. I bought a couple of drinks and Joe seemed to feel better.

I took a break around eight-thirty and went to sit with Connie. We didn't talk. We just sat there, both of us staring at nothing and after ten minutes I went back to work. It wasn't till twenty minutes after nine that the telephone rang at the end of the bar.

Joe answered it. I finished the number I was playing and he nodded at me. I stepped down and walked across the room to the phone. When I looked at Connie, I saw that she hadn't stood up. She had only rolled her head around and was staring at me as I picked up the receiver.

It was Sam Freed's voice.

"The agent is here in my office. You want to bring the girl over?"

"Yeah," I said and hung up.

I beckoned to Connie. She got up and came to the bar. I told Joe we were going out for a breath of air. I took Connie's hand and we went out the back door at the end of the hall and into the alley. We walked hand in hand, without talking, to the next street, turned, and came to Freed's place.

Freed was at his desk and there was a young guy in a business suit in a chair beside him. Freed didn't make any introductions. He nodded us into the chairs. Connie sat on the edge of hers with her hands in her lap.

"Will you tell this man," Freed said to me, "what you told me this morning?"

I went through it again. The F.B.I. agent listened impassively till I got through. When I finished, he thought it over for a minute and then he said, "We checked on that carnival Mr. Freed told us about. There were no such people as you mentioned."

"They probably didn't hang around after Connie left them."

"We're looking for them," he said.

He turned to Freed.

"About those markings on the girl's body—"

"I'll call my wife," Freed said.

He got up and went to a door that led into the house. He opened it and called. A woman came in, smiling. She was a sweet-faced, motherly kind of woman and she went over to Connie right away.

"Would you let Mrs. Freed examine you?" the agent asked Connie.

Connie nodded and got up. The deputy's wife put her arm around Connie's shoulders and led her to the connecting door and through it into the house. The door closed behind them. I looked at Freed and at the agent. Nobody said anything. Then I said, "What happens if you think maybe she's the real Constance Jordan?"

He looked me over briefly and lit a cigarette. He spoke through the smoke.

"I send a report to Los Angeles," he said. "I sent a preliminary report this morning, right after I talked to Mr. Freed."

"Then what?" I said.

He shrugged.

"Then it's up to the courts."

"How about the remains they found at San Bernardino?"

He shrugged again.

"A local coroner's report and a check by the L.A. office. You couldn't determine much. Eight years is a long time."

I noticed that Freed was staring at me with that poker face of his and I began to get nervous. I stood up and nodded to them.

"I've got to get back to work," I said. "Will you escort her back to the hotel when you're through?"

"If she wants to go back there," the agent said.

I went to the door. Freed came along with me. As I opened the door he said, "You say you picked the girl up along the railroad?"

"That's right."

"Where did you come from? Where were you before you got to where she was?"

"Somewhere in Ohio," I said. "I forgot the name of the place."

"Playin' the piano there, were you?"

"Just passing through," I said.

Finally he nodded and stepped back so I could leave.

"I'll see the girl gets back to the hotel," he said.

"Thank you," I said.

Walking back to the hotel I began to think what a nosy bastard he was. Twice he'd asked me where I was working and at what. What difference did it make to him? Connie was the figure in the case. I was just going along for the ride.

There was a good crowd in the Zephyr Room. Most of the tables were filled. There were a couple of empty seats at the bar. I had emptied the kitty when I'd left earlier and now I put a dollar bill back into it, sat down and started to play. I began to get a few requests, which was a good thing, though the customers didn't always pay for them. Some of them did, though, and I had picked up several bills and a lot of loose change at the end of forty-five minutes. It was at about that time, the guy with the scar came in and sat down at the bar.

I don't think I'd have noticed him if I hadn't been keyed up to begin with and if he hadn't looked a little different from anybody else in the room—different the way a man from the city looks among a crowd of small-town people. It was only a small difference, but it was there. He had walked in casually and gone straight to the bar. When he moved it was with economy, as if he liked to save his energy. He wore an expensive, dark felt hat and his shoulders were wide under it. He sat with his back to me and I didn't see his face at first, not till he turned once and glanced back toward the piano. A ray of light from a wall fixture struck his face then and I saw the scar. It wasn't a big scar, but it showed up in the light as a thin white line against his dark face. I saw that his hands were big, the highball glass he held was barely visible when he raised it to his mouth.

I looked away when he glanced toward me and only looked at him again after he'd turned back to the bar. I studied him, trying to figure out what particular thing had made him seem different from the others in the room. I couldn't put a finger on it. It was there all right—the difference—maybe in the way he carried himself, a kind of self-sufficiency—but I couldn't put a name to it. I gave up trying finally, because they were shooting requests at me and I had to pay some attention to the customers. I had a bus ticket at stake.

I worked hard for fifteen more minutes and just as I had decided to take a break, some mousy blonde about fifty weaved her way to the piano and begged me to play "Tenderly" just for her. I saw that she held a crumpled bill in her hand. It looked like a five. I had rendered "Tenderly" at least six times within two hours, but for five bucks I figured I could do it once more. I gave her a smile and started in and she dropped the five-dollar bill into the kitty and then stood there, clinging to the piano while I played it.

I glanced over her shoulder and saw Connie and Sam Freed, the deputy, walking down the corridor toward the service door. Connie stopped in the doorway, looking for me. I waved at her and pointed with my finger toward the room. She went away then, with Freed following her. So I felt better and gave the blonde a real thrill on the last chorus of "Tenderly." I even began to sound good to me. When I finished I gave her that smile again and stood up. But she caught my sleeve and I found out she expected more for her money. I sat down once more and played a quick, easy arrangement of "Body and Soul."

The scar-faced stranger got up and moved along the bar. At the service door he turned through it, into the rear corridor, heading toward the back. It was a funny way to leave the place. In going, he had brushed past Sam Freed, who was standing in the doorway, looking at me. I guessed he'd been there for some time.

After a while he came in and went to the end of the bar near the telephone. I watched him as I finished the piece I was playing. The blonde gushed over it some and started telling me the history of her sad life, which was like all the other lives I had ever heard about, except that the names were different. Still, even some of them were the same—names like Fred, Tom, Jack. I listened till I couldn't hear her any more, then I turned on the smile once and stood up with an air of finality. I emptied the kitty into my hand and stuffed the money in my pocket. She was still talking when I left.

Sam Freed was having a bottle of beer. He put out a hand as I came abreast of him and I moved in beside him at the bar.

"What did the F.B.I. think?" I asked him.

He shrugged. "I don't know. They don't talk much." He finished his beer. "When did you get in town, son?"

"Yesterday."

"Where'd you say you come from?"

"I didn't say."

I offered to buy him a drink and he shook his head, looked at a wrist watch on his arm.

"I'm expecting somebody," he said slowly, "from out of town."

He started away, then turned back.

"You and the girl," he said, "stick around, huh? Till I hear from the F.B.I."

"Sure," I said.

He walked off toward the lobby stairs. I waited till he disappeared, then left the bar and went down to our room.

Light showed under the door. I didn't hear anybody talking. I stood outside with my hand on the knob for a moment, then I twisted it and pushed on in.

The guy with the scar was sitting on the edge of the bed and Connie stood in front of him, with her back to him and her dress pulled up around her waist.

CHAPTER 8

I stood with my back against the closed door. They had both looked up when I came in and after a minute, Connie dropped her dress and came to me. Her face was alive and happy, but I tried to ignore that. I felt outraged and protective.

"Chris," she said, putting her little hands on my chest, "this man has come to take me home."

I looked past her at him.

"That's the way he gets you home?" I said, "by looking at your bare behind?"

The man on the bed laughed easily, relaxed. The scar was plainer now, a thin white line running crookedly down alongside his nose.

"Just a routine check," he said. "Identification—" Finally I looked at Connie.

"When are you leaving?" I asked.

"Right away," she said. "Jeanie sent him for me. It's like you said it would be, Chris!"

The man on the bed stood up. He moved like an athlete, with perfect balance. He wasn't a bad-looking guy, in spite of the scar.

But I hated him. He had come to take my problem off my hands and I hated him.

"The identification business works both ways, doesn't it?" I said. "Did he tell you who he is?"

He gave out with that easy laugh again and pulled out a wallet. He handed me an official-looking card. It showed him to be a registered private detective from Los Angeles by the name of Poole—Roger Poole.

I handed the card back to him.

"All right, Mr. Poole," I said. "How about something from Jean Jordan? Something to show who sent you?"

He was relaxed, putting the card back in his wallet. He pulled something else out of it—an envelope like the kind they give you with railroad or airplane tickets.

"Miss Jordan talked to Constance by telephone last night," he said. "This morning she got a message from the F.B.I. in L.A. It appeared that this young lady was probably her sister and she didn't waste any time sending me out here. I flew to Chicago and drove down here this evening. Here are the tickets home—for Los Angeles—two of them."

I took the envelope and looked into it. There was a plane ticket stub from Los Angeles to Chicago and there were two tickets from Chicago to Los Angeles.

I gave back the envelope and muttered something about being too suspicious.

"You're absolutely right," he said. "Wouldn't want it any other way. Miss Jordan and Constance are both indebted to you."

Connie stood there with her hands on my chest. I looked at her brown eyes.

"You see, Chris?" she said. "You told me Jeanie would help me."

"Yeah, kid," I said.

I walked past her to the bed and sat down heavily. I couldn't get used to the idea she might be going. After a minute I got up again and found my bottle. I offered the private eye a drink and he shook his head. I took one myself. I kept thinking about Sam Freed saying, "You and the girl, stick around, huh? Till I hear from the F.B.I." Had this private cop heard from the F.B.I.? When? When would he have had a chance?

"As soon as you can get packed," he said to Connie.

+

"She doesn't have anything to pack," I said. "She's ready. Did her sister send any money for expenses?"

"Oh, sure," he said, digging into his wallet again. "I almost forgot."

He pulled out five twenties and handed them to Connie. She looked at them in her hand and then at me. She seemed bewildered.

"It's money," I said. "Say thank you to the man."

"Thank you," she said.

Roger Poole cleared his throat and squared his shoulders. They were big shoulders. I sat there watching him and tried to figure out what made him seem so phony. It was the same kind of thing I'd noticed at the bar—nothing I could put my finger on. But something. He was phony. I knew he was phony, but I didn't know how I knew and I couldn't have convinced anybody. Maybe he was only phony in a superficial way and, after all, the main thing was to get Connie back home.

"If you're ready, Miss Jordan—" he said to Connie.

Connie was looking at me.

"I'm ready," she said, "but Chris has to go too."

There was a deep silence, during which I looked at Connie and Poole cleared his throat again.

"Well, I'm afraid—" he said. "I only have the two tickets."

"But Chris has to go," Connie said.

"Miss Jordan didn't know about him," Poole said. "She didn't anticipate sending his transportation."

This was believable enough, but Poole wasn't smiling with his face now. It was set and watchful. I knew he didn't want me to go.

"Is there any reason I *shouldn't* go to Los Angeles?" I said.

He shrugged his big shoulders and shifted his weight.

"Of course not," he said.

I glanced at Connie.

"Of course," I said, "I don't have the money to buy myself a ticket."

That worked fine. Connie walked straight to me and held out the five twenties he'd given her.

"I have," she said. "Here, Chris." She turned to Poole. "Now Chris can buy a ticket and go with us."

He didn't like it. He didn't like it at all. I could see him not liking it and I thought I could begin to see a lot that I hadn't seen before, though I'd been looking hard enough. And the main thing I could see was that he had got here too soon. He was just too damned prompt.

I could also see into the future. I could see Connie going out of this room with him—maybe even getting on a plane with him. But I couldn't see her getting off the plane with him in Los Angeles. All I could see was him getting off alone. I didn't know what would happen along the way, but something would happen. Something had to happen. Because if this skinny kid with the big brown eyes was really Constance Jordan, then she was "hot"—hotter than the hinges. And also because the big money just doesn't move that fast to split itself up.

So Poole stood there, not liking it, but not knowing quite what to do about it either. I could help him, or I could let him sweat it out. Connie was looking first at him, then at me, probably wondering why we didn't get started. There was no way I could tell her why.

Poole didn't sweat very long. He made a hunching movement with his shoulders.

"My car is in the filling station down the street," he said. "Shall we walk up there?"

I had to have a little time. I felt desperate for time. I untied my shoes, started to take them off.

"Why don't you go get it?" I said. "I need a shower. Ten, fifteen minutes. We'll be ready."

He hesitated. He glanced at Connie, then gave me a long, hard look. Then he shrugged.

"All right," he said finally.

He went out. I got the one shoe back on and retied them both. I went to the door and listened till I heard the big steel door at the end of the corridor clang softly shut. Connie was staring at me, her face still shining and happy.

"Chris—" she said.

"We're not going with him," I said.

I looked away from the hurt in her face as it crumpled—the little-girl face that had lived through so much hell and would have to live through a little more—and why? Because a broken-down lush was afflicted with hunches.

But not all hunch either. It wasn't crystal ball stuff. If Poole had a legitimate errand, he'd have got in touch with us through the local law.

"Wait here," I said to her. "I know what I'm doing. Please don't go out of here with anybody till I get back."

I went fast into the Zephyr Room and to the telephone on the wall. I got Sam Freed's number and waited with my fingers crossed till he came on. I told him who I was. When he spoke again his voice was cold and stiff.

"A private cop from Los Angeles," I said, "a guy named Poole. Did he get in touch with you—about taking the Jordan girl home?"

There was a short pause, then he said, "No. You'd better send her up here. We can put her up for a couple of days."

"She's all right where she is," I said.

"Listen, Cross," he said, "I have to tell you—" But I hung up. I'd heard all I wanted to hear. I went back past the bar, not looking at Joe, into the corridor and back into the room. Connie was standing in the middle of it where I had left her.

"Chris, why aren't we going with the man?" she said. "He's got the tickets and everything—"

"Baby," I said, "I can't tell you right now. Try to string along. We'll leave here right now if you're ready."

"But, I don't—" I took her arm. She came along reluctantly. I reached for the light switch beside the door and the door opened, suddenly and wide. I cursed myself for taking time to phone, giving Poole a chance to get back.

Then I saw that the guy who stood in the door, blocking most of it with wide, sloping shoulders, peering into the room with his low-browed, ugly face, was not Poole. It was Danny, the "pig," the redhead's husband from back in Ohio. I saw, too, why Sam Freed had asked me so many questions and why his voice sounded cold and distant.

But there wasn't time to think about that. Danny Boy was coming into the room, pushing the door shut behind him with his foot.

Connie backed clear across the room to the wall, her hands covering her mouth. I think she thought at first it was Kretch, come to get her.

But the big ape paid no attention to her. His eyes were on me and they weren't full of love.

"The sheriff said I'd find you here," he said. "You want to ask the lady to leave?"

His voice was grating and rough, as I remembered it. I had never got a good, clear look at him in daylight, so I had forgotten how big he was. I couldn't see any way to get through that door without an All-American tackle to block him out. But I tried to bluff it through.

"The lady stays," I said, "and you go."

He didn't laugh. He just went over me again with his little eyes. He took a couple of slow, shuffling steps toward me. I backed away. I backed into the bedside table and my whisky bottle rattled behind me. I had used the same thing on his wife once. Maybe I could use it on him. Anyway, it was all I had.

I reached back and got a grip on it. I twisted just far enough to grab the bottle and smash its neck against the table, then swung back to face Danny holding the jagged end in front of me.

He stopped. There were five or six feet between us.

"Come on," I said. "Rush me. Just once."

Even he was smart enough not to do that. He stepped back. His right hand started a fast trip toward his chest and I didn't wait to find out what kind of gun he had. I slammed the bottle into his face. He threw up both hands and roared, charging blind at the same time. I jumped out of the way and he crashed into the bedside table, then fell across the bed. I knew he wouldn't stay there long. The glass hadn't cut him.

I grabbed one of his feet and twisted it sharply. He kicked me in the stomach and I sat down on the floor. I reached for the bottle and we got to our feet at the same time. He swung the little table up with the legs aimed at me and came on. The legs were far enough apart to go past me on both sides and I braced myself and took the shock, then hit him on the side of his head with the bottle. He dropped the table and reeled away from me.

It was just one crazy break after another and I knew it couldn't last. When he came up against the wall he reached for the gun again and I threw the bottle once more, broken end first. This time it cut him. Blood flowed out of his cheek. He cursed me and wiped his face with his hand. I was out of weapons. He was standing straight with his back against the wall. I lowered my head and ran at him, butting him with my head in his belly. His breath gasped out of him and he sagged down on top of me.

I had aimed too high when I hit him and his belt buckle stunned me and cut my head. I didn't go clear out but it took what seemed a long time to untangle myself and crawl out from under him. He was still moving on the floor, holding himself with both hands and I had time to find the bottle and hit him in the head with it until he lay still. One of his feet was under the bed.

I got up, rubbing my head and Connie was still standing with her hands over her mouth, her brown eyes wide and terrified.

"We've got to get out of here," I said.

I took her arm and let her into the corridor. I reasoned that even if Poole drove into the alley, he'd have to go to the front of the hotel to get in. The service door was locked at night.

The hell with him. He could come back and revive Danny Boy and the two of them could have a nice long talk.

I pulled Connie along to the back door. She didn't want to come. She'd been all set to go with Poole back to Los Angeles and Jeanie. How could I explain to her that she'd never make it that way? Answer: I couldn't.

I opened the door and looked into the alley. There were no cars in sight. It was only a short distance to the next street toward the south of town and I figured south was the direction for us to go. I had guessed, by the route of the railroad by which we had come to town, that the road to Chicago would be to the north and west.

Connie stopped and braced her feet, pulling back. I turned to face her.

"Chris," she said. "I want to go back with Mr. Poole. Why can't we?"

For a moment I gave up. I thought, why go on with it? If she wants to go, let her go. She can have a little trip with Poole and I can go back and have a drink or two and kick Danny Boy in the face every time he comes around. It would be so much more peaceful that way.

But I knew I couldn't do it. I knew I would only go back and sit and think about Connie and wonder where she was and the time would come when I couldn't drink enough to forget it. I had to try once more.

"Listen, honey," I said, "we've come a long way so far. You don't know how far I've come. It's no time to quit. We'll get back to Los Angeles all right, but we'll get back our way. So we'll be sure. Because, believe me, Mr. Poole is a phony."

"But I don't understand, Chris—"

"I hope you never do," I said. "But right now, I hope you'll come along on faith. I'll get you to L.A."

She stood there in the alley, her face white against the dark of the building wall. She looked at me for a long time. And finally she moved a little way toward me and her voice was flat and I knew the happiness she'd felt half an hour before, when I'd walked in and found her showing the birthmark to Poole, was gone. I wondered whether it would ever come back.

"All right," she said dully, "I'll go."

Headlights swung into the alley from beyond the hotel and bore down on us. I pulled Connie back into a doorway and held on, trying to figure out what I would do if it were Poole and if he had seen us. But the lights went on past and I saw it was a delivery truck. I waited till it had turned into the next street and disappeared.

Then we went on down the alley to the street and turned toward the town's main drag. It was too soon to expect anything from Danny or Sam Freed. Certainly Poole would waste some time after he got back to the room and found Danny laid out and waiting. So I figured we would have time to get to the river before anybody started after us.

Connie didn't protest any more. She didn't say anything at all. She just came along with me. I pushed the pace pretty hard all the way to the railroad tracks and by that time we were well out of the lighted area of the main street. Across the tracks, the street became a country road, curving to cross a bridge over the river, and disappearing among the woodplots ahead. At the bridge we went down the bank and walked along the river.

I was so anxious to leave the town that I didn't notice how Connie was dropping behind. I stopped finally and she was leaning against a tree, her head back; her breath coming in gasps.

"I'm sorry," I said. "We'll rest."

She didn't answer. I waited till she was breathing more easily, then took her hand and we went on more slowly. We came to another bridge and climbed up to the road. A field of new-mown hay bordered the river on the opposite side.

We crossed the bridge and I found a place in the fence where we could crawl through. I held it for Connie and then followed her. I stopped her beside a pile of hay and began making a couple of beds.

When I had one of the piles set up, I motioned to Connie and she lay down on it. I covered her with the hay and made up a bed for myself. I lay down, but I didn't go to sleep right away. I lay and looked at the sky and smelled the sweet, fresh hay and after a while I heard the far-off rumble of a train coming toward us from the southeast, another like the one Connie and I had ridden that first night. It came slowly, shuddering along the track and then, as it passed us, it roared and pounded for a while and passed on. I settled down into the hay. It seemed like a long, long way to Los Angeles.

CHAPTER 9

We walked most of the next day, but not on the soft ground by the water. A dirt road wound through the countryside, following the course of the river, and it made walking easier. Every hour or so there would be a car or a farm truck on the road and a couple of times we got short rides, ten or fifteen miles each. It helped.

The men who picked us up, both of them farmers, asked a few questions, but I put them off. They weren't unfriendly and I never gave them a chance to get suspicious. They both eyed Connie plenty, but they didn't try anything.

I asked a few questions myself and found that we were bearing southwest and would pass through no cities as long as we stayed on this route. Now and then we crossed a main highway, but the road by the river never joined any of them and it seemed to go on forever.

Late in the afternoon, a guy stopped and offered us a ride clear to the Mississippi River, across from Hannibal, Missouri. He figured on getting there about ten o'clock that night. It was a good offer and we climbed in. He had a big new car and he didn't hesitate to push it.

He asked a couple of routine questions, such as where are you going, and how far have you come? I made up some routine answers, such as "going to the Coast" and "came from back up the road," and he didn't pry any. Connie fell asleep and he suggested she could lie down in the back. So she climbed back there and the driver and I rode along in the front seat. He pointed it out to me when we crossed the state line into Illinois.

We stopped for a quick meal in a little hamlet somewhere and he offered to pay for it, but I didn't let him. I had the hundred dollars Poole had given Connie and some more besides—about a hundred and twenty-five altogether. I didn't pull any of the twenties out of my pocket. Not that I didn't trust the guy, but it might look funny for us to be hitchhiking with a pocketful of dough like that.

I kept thinking that if Poole had been on the level and Jean Jordan had really sent for her sister, then I was in a hell of a position. I had not only thwarted her sister's good intentions, but I had actually kidnapped the girl myself and was now taking her with me across state lines.

The F.B.I. had already reported on her. An F.B.I. man had seen the two of us together, had known we were living at the hotel in Westbrook, Indiana. If Danny should go back and report to Sam Freed, and if Poole should report to him too, they would have the F.B.I. after us within minutes. And they would know whom to look for.

But I had gambled that Poole was not on the level. And I gambled too that Danny had come to get me himself, after giving Freed some cock-and-bull story in order to locate me, because Danny didn't want the law fooling around with his revenge.

So if they were both doing what I suspected, we had a chance—that is, I had a chance. Connie was in the clear. I was very curious to know whether the F.B.I. had been notified about us. If they had, it would probably be in the headlines, because the heiress to the Jordan fortune would be big news. If it was not in the news, the chances were good that the F.B.I. was not looking for us and that I had guessed right about Poole.

Connie had gone to sleep again in the back seat and around eight o'clock the guy leaned over and turned on his radio.

"Time for news," he said.

That was all right with me. I listened to every word. There were a lot of words, because the newscast went on for fifteen minutes. But there were no words about Constance Jordan or a piano player named Cross or about the F.B.I. None whatever. I leaned back in the seat and relaxed and the man who drove the car found some music and turned it down low and we rode through the peaceful Illinois countryside, behind little, lighted towns, and at about ten o'clock that night, just as he had figured, he pulled up by the Mississippi River and pointed out the bridge that crossed it into Hannibal.

"I think you could get a bus to get across," he said, and told me where to go.

I woke Connie and thanked him and we watched while he drove away. There was a filling station near where we had stopped and I went over there and borrowed a map of Missouri. I found that we could angle south and west from Hannibal and get to Kansas City. From Kansas City, I was sure we could get a ride to Los Angeles without having to use the so-called common carriers.

Connie was groggy from the sleep and the strain of the last two days and she came along with me like a child. I stopped in a liquor store and bought a pint bottle and put it in my pocket. I hadn't had a drink all day except for a bottle of beer at lunch and another when we stopped for dinner. I wanted a drink very much. But I was surprised at how good I felt without it. I didn't trust the feeling, but I figured I would try to go along with it for a while and see what happened. Still, it would be good to have the bottle, just in case.

We found a bus that would take us across the river and through Hannibal to the west side of town. It was a long, slow ride. Connie fell asleep again and I had to waken her when it was time to get off. She stumbled, climbing down, and I caught her, and after the bus moved away she sat down limply on a bench at the stop and just shook her head.

"I'm too tired, Chris," she said. "I can't walk anymore."

I picked her up off the bench and started down the street, carrying her. She was light in my arms and it wasn't hard going. The bus stop was in the outskirts of town and I could see that the lights stopped only a few blocks ahead. We could find a place to stop for the night as soon as we got into the country.

I carried her three blocks and then the sidewalk ended. I walked along a dirt path beside the highway, looking for a hayfield. It didn't take long to find one. There was no fence and I walked back into it, away from the road, and found a pile of hay. I laid Connie on it and covered her and then I made a pile for myself and sat down and took off my shoes. It was another warm summer night and the traffic, except for the trucks, was only a faint purr on the highway.

My hand brushed against the bulge in my pocket where I'd put the bottle. I started to draw it out, then dropped it.

If I take one now, I thought, I'll take it all. Maybe I wouldn't like all of it. Maybe I'm getting bigger than the bottle. I felt full of accomplishment and promise and a little proud of myself. I looked at Connie, asleep on the hay, and thought, we've come a long way. Have I brought you, or have you brought me?

I stretched out and looked at the sky again, as I had the night before. This was a better night. Things had begun to happen inside me, things I couldn't name, but which were good things. Today, I thought, was a damn near perfect day.

And I was damn near right. It had been a good day and it might have been a good night, except for one thing.

Connie ran away.

* * * *

I don't know how long I slept. I'd been restless and uncomfortable in the hay, then suddenly I was wide awake, staring at the sky and it was still dark. I lay still for a few minutes, wondering what made me restless, and finally I turned my head to look for Connie on the other pile of hay. Mine was lower and I couldn't see whether she had maybe rolled off, or had sunk down below sight. I got up slowly, walked over to the other hay mound and looked down. Connie wasn't there.

I grew cold and stiff inside. I turned around slowly, gazing out over the field as I turned, and then I pulled out the pint bottle, tore the wrapping from around the cap, unscrewed it and took a long drink. For a minute, then, I felt warmer on the inside. But there was a hard knot growing in my stomach, creeping up toward my chest. Because it was night, and we'd come this far, and now she was gone.

She wouldn't do it, I thought. She wouldn't go off like that—not unless someone had forced her to go. She wouldn't run out that way.

But clearly, she had gone. I wouldn't get anywhere arguing with myself. I would have to find her—soon and safe.

And what if I didn't find her? I asked myself. And I couldn't stand it to think of an answer.

I forced myself to stand still and think. She wouldn't have left without some idea about where she was going. So she wouldn't have gone back farther into the field. There was nowhere back there to go, except maybe to somebody's farmhouse. If she went to the highway and stuck her thumb in the air, it wouldn't be long before somebody would stop and give her a lift.

I ran across the field toward the highway. The tough hay stubble came through the holes in my shoes, but I couldn't feel it then. As I ran I thought it was most likely she would go back to town and find a telephone. Suddenly I stopped short and put my hand in my pocket. I felt the bills. I pulled them out and counted them in the dark, feeling them. It was all there. So she didn't have any money.

I came to the edge of the field and fell into the ditch beside the highway. A truck rumbled by over my head while I picked myself up and felt to make sure I hadn't lost the bottle. I climbed to the shoulder beside the pavement and started back toward the town. The truck traffic was heavy and they came at me one after another, the white glare of the lights blinding me each time. I stopped and took another pull from the bottle.

The rumble of the heavy trucks and the roar of their motors was like something solid against my ears. I began to panic. She might have run onto the highway and been struck down. God knew how far she would have gone before it happened. It could have happened and I would never know about it the rest of my life.

I turned my back on the road and went into the field again. I waited for a lull in the traffic, then cupped my mouth with my hands and shouted her name. I shouted it over and over. Most of the time the trucks drowned it out. Pretty soon I was hoarse. I couldn't even hear myself when I shouted. I took another drink and it helped for a little while, but then the hoarseness came back again.

The hayfield ended and I stopped, leaning against a post, trying to catch my breath. I took another drink and saw that the bottle was half-empty.

I looked back over the field I had crossed, and began to laugh out loud.

She's gone. Understand? She's lammed out, ducked, taken a powder.

Why not? I thought. I'm as phony as all the rest. I've been giving myself this big build-up. Noble. Only thinking of Connie. Protecting her. I talked myself into it so good that when a guy shows up with plane tickets to take her home, I figure *he's* a phony. Then I go right on selling myself. Only I—Christopher Cross—am on the level. I'm the only one in the wide world who can get her home safe. Guys who think like that wind up making baskets in white-walled rooms. To wired music.

What's the truth? I thought. What's the real reason I wouldn't let her go? The real reason is very simple. I figured that maybe after all she is really Constance Jordan. So she's got a million bucks. I figured that if I'm the one that brings her back, I can get a piece of that big money. Besides that—maybe—after she fills out and quiets down, I can get a piece of her personally. Me, hero, with a big objective: spend the money and lay the girl. Free enterprise. You see your opportunity and you grab it.

And she figured it out, in her little-girl mind, and naturally she ran away. So let her go, Chris, and shove off, push along, hit the road. At least you got a hundred bucks out of the deal and she'll probably never come back for it.

I folded my hands against the fence post and laid my head on them. I was what they call "all gone" in the middle. I couldn't push along any farther without some more sleep. Somewhere in this big field of hay, I had made a bed. It seemed important that I go back to it. None other would do.

I lowered the level of whisky in my bottle another half-inch and replaced it in my pocket. I began looking around for the two mounds of hay I had kicked into beds—one for her and one for me. There would be a deep depression in mine and a shallower one in hers. Maybe mine would still be warm. Maybe hers too. Maybe I would finish out the night in hers. There might be a trace of her left in it, a scent, an essence. I coughed, choking. Essence of a million dollars. How does it feel, I wondered, to sleep with money?

It was a long time before the idea went through my head that I probably wouldn't be able to find the bed I'd made. It was a big field. There was no moon. The faint starlight showed the hay mounds like dark lumps against the darker ground. There must be a million of them. I hadn't taken any sightings when we stopped for the night. When I'd found her gone and run madly to the highway, I hadn't bothered to pick out any landmarks. How in hell would I find my way to two particular mounds, when from here they all looked alike?

I had to find them. Panic began welling up in me again as I realized that nothing was more important than those two mounds of hay. They were as important as food, as the bottle in my pocket, as important as music.

I began running, jerkily, pausing at each mound to examine it, feel it with my hands, sniffing it. I didn't pay any attention to where I was running. The sounds of the highway traffic faded behind me. I could tell when a truck passed, but the roar of it no longer beat against my head. I ran out of breath and stopped to look around and I saw I was far back from the road. Too far. We hadn't come this far. We'd made our beds closer to the highway.

I took a couple of steps toward the road and my legs gave out. The running, the shouting and panic had caught up with me. I couldn't move. I fell across a hay mound with my face in my arms and I didn't care if I never got up.

I lay like that for a long time and then my arms and legs began to tingle, ache and finally shoot with sharp pain. I stood up and walked around for a few minutes to remove the pain. I had another drink and sat down on the hay.

There was less traffic now. A truck would pass, then it would be a long, time before another came along. In between, there was deep silence. Sometimes a cricket would break in, once in a while a night bird. Twice I thought I heard a cat screaming in that horrifying, half-human way they have.

After a while I heard another sound, not a cricket nor a bird. Not quite like a cat either, but thin and high like that. But my senses had begun to dull again and I didn't pay much attention. I sat there, blinking, while another truck passed, and made a big thing out of trying to decide whether to go to sleep or get up and move on. I didn't want to sleep right here. I had made a familiar bed and I hated the thought of sleeping in a strange one.

Then it came again, the new sound, a little closer now, and louder. Something in it brought me to my feet. I listened, hoping it would come again, needing to hear it again. It came and I thought it had come from the far corner of the field toward the highway. I took a few steps and paused to listen again. It didn't come. I took a few more and heard it while I was walking. It was farther away. I'd been wrong about the direction. I shifted, ran a few steps. I stopped again and listened. Then I shouted.

"Connie!" I waited and shouted once more. "Conneee!"

Right away I heard an answer. Still far-off, but pointed now at me, toward where I stood. I shouted again and she answered again and I thought I had it placed. I ran toward the sound over the sharp hay stubble, dodging the mounds that loomed up every few feet. She called again and I shifted my direction, ran faster. Once I fell down and when I got up I had lost my way again and I called her. This time, when she answered, she was nearer.

Then I saw her, near the middle of the big field, far back from the hayfield, running, a faint white flashing in the dark.

We stopped running at the same time and there was a mound of hay between us. We stood, staring at each other across it. Then Connie spoke.

"Chris—" I walked onto the mound and over it toward her. She fell against me and slipped to her knees. I lifted her and led her back to the mound and we sat down on it. Her arms were around my neck, thin and tight. She was shaking and she made little sobbing sounds as she fought for breath. My own breath was too thin for talking. I held her in both arms and she didn't feel like a million dollars. She felt like a lost girl in a hayfield under the sky. She felt like home.

I don't know how long I held her that way, with her arms around my neck and her head against my chest. I know that she found her voice first.

"I got scared, Chris," she said. "I woke up and couldn't go back to sleep. I thought about you. I didn't know anything about you. I didn't know whether we were going to Los Angeles or somewhere else. I thought about Jeanie and Mr. Poole and how you wouldn't let me go with him."

"Baby—" I said.

"I thought about how it was with Madeleine and Kretch, sleeping in the tent, and the men—and I thought about you in the hotel the other night. I was scared. I thought I had to get away from you if I ever wanted to get home. I could go down to the road and get a ride, I thought."

She had begun to sob again, violently, in my arms, her small body shuddering. I held her more closely, ran my fingers through her long, dark hair.

"But the trucks kept coming, Chris. They scared me too. I walked along the road, but I couldn't walk all the way home. I couldn't walk any more, Chris."

"You don't have to walk any more, Connie."

"I started back. I found the field all right. I knew that's where we had stayed. But I couldn't remember where you were. I walked all over looking for you. I kept calling you, but you didn't answer."

I stroked her hair, trying to find some words. There weren't any.

"I won't run away again, Chris."

I thought of a word finally. It was her name. But it drowned in my throat. I held her and rocked a little back and forth and gradually her sobbing quieted and then stopped. I eased her arms off the back of my neck, got up and began making a couple of beds out of the hay mound. I picked her up and carried her to one of the beds I'd made and began to cover her with hay. She put a hand up to my face and I felt how cold she was. I lay down beside her and pulled hay over the two of us. She lay in my arms, clinging to me with her whole body, and we began to create warmth between us.

"We're both running away, Connie," I said. "We don't have to run away forever. I found something out, I think. Anyway something about me. What I've been running away from is something I really want. I had it once and I lost it. But it doesn't have to stay lost."

I looked at the sky. I felt Connie, warm against me. I felt whatever it is that goes back and forth between two people when they begin making something together.

"I was a great pianist once, Connie," I said. "It's something you can feel, but nobody has to tell you. Maybe I can be great again. I began to feel it the other night. I didn't trust it. But maybe now it's true. Maybe, if I try, I can do it again…"

Connie didn't answer. I listened to the sound of her breathing, moved an arm gently. She settled closer against me. She was asleep.

CHAPTER 10

In the morning we walked back into Hannibal and had breakfast in a little café near the edge of town. Connie was drawn and tired-looking, but after she'd had a chance to clean up and a good meal, she rallied and was cheerful—more cheerful than she had been since I'd met her.

We found we could get a Greyhound bus to Kansas City that would get us there early in the evening. The bus trip was long and hot, but we slept off and on, and by the time we pulled into Kansas City, after dark, it had cooled off. I remembered a low-priced hotel downtown from my touring days with the band, and we went in there and got a room with twin beds. I bought a couple of newspapers and we went up to the room. Connie went to bed and I opened the papers to the classified sections and studied them until I found what I wanted.

The ad read: "Los Angeles. Share expenses. Three pass." There was a phone number to call. It was a commercial deal really and I knew it. You paid a flat fee and the driver took a carful of people to Los Angeles. It was illegal, but it was cheaper than train or bus and there wouldn't be any wasted time. There wouldn't be any overnight stops.

I called the number in the ad and whoever answered said he had room for two more and would pick us up at the hotel in the morning around ten. The "expenses" would come to twenty-five dollars apiece. I said we'd be ready.

I counted the money I had left. We'd have about forty-five bucks after paying for the ride. If we were careful, we could get along for a couple days in L.A. while Connie got established and I looked for a job.

When I went to bed I had a good, strong feeling. I still had some whisky in the bottle I'd bought in Hannibal, but I forgot to take a drink from it. I hit the bed and went to sleep.

The next morning we stood in the hot sun in front of the hotel, waiting for the car to pick us up. It was half an hour late. It was a medium-heavy car, in good shape, and I thought the long ride wouldn't be too rugged.

The other passengers were all right. There was a middle-aged lady with gray hair who sat in front most of the way, and a Marine sergeant returning to San Diego from a furlough. The driver was an expert, the conversation was casual and not too steady, and by the time we got onto the sun-baked Kansas plains everybody was well shaken down and Connie and I settled in to the long ride.

Because it was long. Long and hot and nerve-shattering. The driver gave out somewhere in New Mexico and the sergeant spelled him until he went to sleep. I took a turn at it, but I went to sleep three times and nearly ran us into a truck, so the driver took over again. We began to stop every couple of hours for coffee and food. Most of these times, Connie stayed in the car and slept, but I made her get out at least four times a day and eat something. There were dark circles under her eyes and her skin seemed to grow paler all the time.

I had started taking a drink now and then as far back as Texas, and by the time we reached western Arizona, I was taking more and more. I knew the driver didn't like it, but he didn't make any direct complaint till we stopped, late one night, in Prescott, Arizona. We all got out except Connie. The driver and the lady in the front seat went into a café for coffee. I invited the sergeant to have a drink with me in the adjoining bar and we went in there.

We stayed longer than we'd planned. I bought him a drink and he returned it, then I bought him another and he had to go another round. We were groggy from lack of sleep and I was getting pretty high on the drinks. When we finally heard the horn that was honking outside, we sat there at the bar and tried to talk ourselves into thinking it was for somebody else.

The Marine gave in first and got down and I followed him outside. The car was parked into the curb and the driver got out of it and walked over to meet us. The sergeant walked around him and went on to the car. The driver stopped me with a hand on my arm.

"Look," he said, "I got enough to do to drive, without playing nursemaid to a lush. I figured you for one in Kansas City, but I thought I'd take a chance."

I'd had just enough to feel mildly belligerent.

"Relax," I said. "It's a free country."

"Maybe," he said. "But in a few hours, bud, we're coming to California. They've got an inspection station and we have to stop. If they figure I'm hauling passengers for pay, I can get in the kind of trouble I don't want any of. With you drunk, I don't like the picture."

A door opened in the car and Connie climbed out. I saw her walking toward us and I tried to walk past the driver, to get back in the car before it went any further. But he stopped me again.

"How about it?" he said. "You going to behave yourself?"

I couldn't take the pushing around.

"You do the driving," I said. "I'll take care of myself."

He gave me a hard look.

"See that you do," he said. "Or you'll walk the rest of the way to Los Angeles."

Suddenly Connie was between us, pounding her small fists on his chest.

"Don't talk to him like that!" she said. "Stop it!"

The guy was pretty bewildered. He backed off a little, trying to catch Connie's fists with his hands.

"You can't talk to him that way!" Connie said.

I put a hand on her shoulder.

"Wait, honey," I said. "It's all right."

She turned to me then and put her face against my chest. The driver looked at us, shaking his head, turned away and went back to the car. Connie and I followed him. The Marine was asleep in the back seat when we got in. Connie put her head on my shoulder and I held her while she slept. I slept on and off myself and when I was awake, I spent most of the time thinking about her, about the sound of her voice and the flashing of those little fists as she'd fought to protect me.

The toughest part of the trip came after we'd got through the inspection station at Blythe and headed across the California wasteland on the last lap. We had struck it early in the morning and as the sun rose, the heat filled the car like something alive, something vindictive. We drove with the windows closed and inside it grew stale and oppressive. But it was better than being whipped and burned by that hot wind. The driver was running on sheer nerve now and I thought, when he staggered out of the car at Indio for one last cup of coffee, that he would give up altogether.

Then we began to climb to the western edge of the desert and pretty soon we were dropping down into Riverside and rolling over the wide highway, past orange groves and sprawling industrial plants, toward Los Angeles' East Side. I looked out at the white houses on the hills and tried to remember what they had looked like the last time I'd seen them. But it was too long ago and too many things had come in between me and the memory. It was another Christopher Cross who was coming home.

Connie stirred sleepily against me, finally lifted her head and looked out the window.

"How long, Chris?" she said.

"We're there, baby," I said. "This is it. The old home town."

She put her fingers on the window ledge and pressed her face against the glass, staring out as we ground through the traffic of the dismal East Side. She asked me what the buildings were at the Civic Center and I told her about some of them, but some I had forgotten.

The driver had to go to Hollywood anyway, so I told him we'd ride to Hollywood and Vine. We let the Marine sergeant out downtown and the gray-haired lady left us somewhere along Wilshire Boulevard. Now that he'd made it, the driver's spirits had picked up and when we got out at the corner of Hollywood and Vine he grinned and we shook hands.

"Thanks for the lift," I said.

"Sorry I had to shoot off my mouth," he said.

"Forget it."

He drove away and lost himself in the traffic.

There was a low-priced commercial hotel within a couple of blocks and we walked over there. I took a room for three days and paid in advance. It left me with about forty dollars cash.

In the room, Connie went to the window and stood there a long time, looking out. I filled the bathtub half full of hot water and told her when it was ready, but she didn't want to leave the window.

"I just want to look at it," she said. "I'm home—almost."

But she swayed on her feet while she said it. I caught her and helped her to the bed. I helped her undress, carried her into the bathroom and put her in the tub. Then I went out to wait for her. I fell asleep waiting and when I woke she still hadn't come out of the bathroom. I knocked on the door, but there was no answer. Finally I went in and she had fallen asleep in the tub. The water was cool. I heated it again and woke her and left again. This time she managed to stay awake long enough to dry herself and come out. I opened the bed for her, she climbed in and I covered her. She murmured at me sleepily.

"Jeanie," she said. "We've got to call Jeanie."

There was a phone by the bed. I picked it up and went through the same long routine we had gone through back in Westbrook, Indiana, to get a connection with the unlisted number. I had to hang up and wait to be called back and while I waited, I fell asleep. When the thing finally rang, a sibilant, Oriental voice said Miss Jordan was not in. The voice went on to tell me that Miss Jordan's attorney was a man named Foster, with an office in Beverly Hills.

I found Foster's number and called it. A girl answered and when I told her Connie Jordan was with me, she said, "Mr. Foster will be in the office tomorrow afternoon. We've been expecting you."

I made an appointment for the next day at two P.M. and hung up the phone.

I was too tired to sleep. Everything in me had cried for sleep for forty-eight hours. But now I couldn't make it. I lay there beside Connie, trying not to turn and toss, and the harder I tried, the more my exhausted nerves screamed for release.

After what seemed like hours I got up, found the pint bottle in my coat and drank some of it. It helped. I took some more and pretty soon I felt drowsy. I had put the bottle away and started to go back to bed when there was a knock on the door.

I stiffened, listening and it came again, sharper, harder.

I glanced at the door and saw it was bolted from the inside. Unless the hotel was on fire, there could be nobody at the door who meant us any good. But I had to know.

The knock came again and I got the bottle and took another long pull. Then I went to the door and spoke softly through the panel.

"Who is it?"

A man's voice answered.

"Police," it said gruffly.

I reached for the knob, then drew back my hand.

"All right," I said. "Shove your badge under the door." There was a long pause. The doorknob rattled. Then he spoke again.

"Open up, Cross."

This time I placed him.

"Poole?" I said. "Leave us alone. I already made a date with Foster."

"That's what I want to talk to you about. So open up."

"The hell with it," I said. "If Foster wants to talk to me, he knows where I am."

"Now look, Cross," he said. "You can't hold the girl that way. Don't be stubborn—" I took a deep breath.

"Give it up," I said. "Leave us alone. If you wake up the kid, I swear to God I'll raise hell. I'll get cops up here—the F.B.I.—everybody! And I don't think you want that."

There was another of those pauses.

"I'm warning you—" he said.

"All right. You did your duty. Now go away."

Behind me I heard Connie move on the bed.

"Beat it," I said through the door panel. "Now!"

I listened. He didn't say any more and he didn't knock. The corridor was carpeted, so I couldn't tell whether he walked away. But if he wanted to stand out there all night, it was up to him. I took one more drink and went to bed.

I had done some big talking—about the F.B.I. and all. But I wasn't so worried about the official law as I was about Poole. It would be a hell of a life if he was going to come around beating on the door at all hours.

Not that it was late. It was around six in the evening. I hoped we would sleep till the next day. I thought Connie could all right, but I wasn't so sure of myself.

Before I dropped off, I made a mental note to call Doc Brockman in the morning.

This guy Philip Brockman was a psychiatrist. We'd got acquainted some years before, when I was playing in this and that joint around Los Angeles. He used to come in to hear me. A real great guy. We were both being divorced at about the same time and after I'd finished work for the night we'd go somewhere and talk or have our own private jam session, sometimes at his place, sometimes at mine. He had a concert grand piano in the living room of a big house in the Wilshire district.

He knew a lot of music. He'd worked his way through medical school playing with dance bands in the East. He no longer played very well when I knew him, but after all, that wasn't his field. We got to be close friends, before I lammed out of town with a bottle under each arm and a headful of bad memories. I had never asked him for a free consultation and he had never used me to furnish free entertainment for his friends—as sometimes happens. He was older than I, but still a young man, very bright, and I guess he had a profitable practice.

He told me some things about my own problems, but not in any professional way. Once in a while he would tell me I'd be better off not to drink so much, but everybody tells you that, and who listens? Maybe if I had stuck around and got to know him even better, he could have helped me. But I don't know. I didn't know then, either, and I don't think he did.

Anyway, I thought of him because he was the only one I could think of, out of all the people I'd known, whom I could really depend on. And there were things I might need, including advice.

For one thing, and soon now, we would have to get around town some and it would be easier if we could have a car. I remembered that the Doc always had two cars and I knew I could ask him for the use of one without hurting anything there was between us.

It was still early in the morning when I called his home. He answered and I told him who I was. He seemed glad to hear from me, and asked how I was doing, when I got back and so on. I put it up to him about a car and he said I was welcome to the Ford convertible that was parked in his garage. There was a set of keys under the hood. He had to leave the office and he would leave the garage unlocked. I thanked him and he said, "Wait. There's a price."

"You're the doctor," I said.

"I've just had the piano tuned."

"Good for you."

"You catch on quick," he said. "I'll be expecting you. Call first."

I didn't like this part of it. I couldn't play anymore the way he would remember. But he had me in a corner.

"I may bring a guest," he said.

"Blonde or brunette?"

"Midnight blue."

He laughed.

"All right, Chris. Maybe I can find a date for myself."

I thanked him again for the car and hung up. Connie was washing out her things. I told her I had to run an errand and would be right back. She didn't say anything, just looked at me flatly. She'd been quiet and depressed all morning.

Maybe, I thought, a person could take only so much—so much brutality, so much hoping, so much waiting. Maybe she'd got to the point where she either had to get something back, something definite, or come apart at the seams. I hoped the attorney, Foster, would be able to settle things in a hurry and get her back where she belonged.

I led her to the door and showed her how to throw the bolt. I made her do it three or four times. Then I made her promise to throw it as soon as I went out and not to open the door for anyone at all until I got back. She promised. I went out then and walked around the corner to the Broadway-Hollywood to wait for a bus.

I was standing there, leaning against the bus stop sign, when this green business coupe went by slowly, close to the curb. There were two men in it and neither was looking at me. I didn't recognize the one on the outside, but the driver was Roger Poole.

I swore out loud. Were they watching me? Or were they just waiting for me to get gone, so they could go to the hotel and pick up Connie?

There was one way to find out. It would cost a little money, but if it worked, it would be worth it.

The green coupe had stopped for a light at the corner. There was a cabstand beside the store on Vine Street and I walked over there fast and got into a cab, directing the driver to the corner of Wilshire and Crenshaw. He started right off and the light changed at the corner. Looking through the rear window, I saw the green coupe slide around the corner and follow us.

Good then. As long as they followed me, they wouldn't bother Connie. I kept watching through the window and pretty soon the driver said, "Somebody tailing you, bud?"

"Yeah," I said, "and that's all right with me."

"Cops?"

"No," I said. "I would like to start losing them at Wilshire." I gave him some directions and Doc Brockman's address. "All right with you?"

"Sure," he said. "A cinch in that neighborhood."

It didn't take long to get to Wilshire and the green coupe was three cars behind us as we approached the light. It had turned to amber and the driver waited till the last possible moment, then swung left into Wilshire, his tires screaming, and when I looked back, the coupe had got hung up on the red signal.

We twisted and turned some in the neighborhood of Wilshire and Crenshaw and finally drew up in front of Doc's house. I paid the driver and let him pull away. Then I went fast up the driveway, opened the garage and got Doc's convertible started.

I was breathing hard and I was scared. We had ditched Poole for now, but no doubt he would head for the hotel. I hoped to get there first.

It didn't take long, and the green coupe was nowhere in sight as I parked the convertible and went into the hotel. Our room was on the second floor and I took the steps rather than wait for the old, creaking elevator. At the room I knocked and waited. After a while I knocked again. I tried the knob and the door was locked. I knocked once more, loudly, and called, "Connie!"

After an endless time her voice came, thin and far-off inside the room. I leaned against the door, panting, and nearly fell into the room when she opened it to let me in.

CHAPTER 11

Foster's office was on the second floor of a Beverly Drive building. There were two girls in the reception office and a third behind a glass window between the reception room and Foster's inner office. When we walked in, one of the receptionists asked us to sit down for a few minutes please. The other got up from her typewriter and went into the secretary's office. While we waited, Connie sat still beside me, her hands tense and stiff in her lap. I couldn't think of anything to say to her.

We waited quite a while and then the secretary rose behind her glass wall, disappeared, reappeared and nodded at us. She didn't smile. I noticed nobody smiled around there.

Connie held back, seemed frightened, and I had to urge her along. She held tightly to my hand as we entered Foster's office. Her hand was cold and damp.

Foster was big, immaculate and somewhat stuffy. He had a "man of distinction" face and thick, slightly graying hair. The skin of his face and the backs of his hands was smooth and carefully sun-tanned. He had a deep, well-trained voice. He shook hands with me, then turned and looked at Connie. He smiled a little, but there was no warmth in it. It was all professional.

"So this is the young lady," he said.

It was a hell of a thing to say and it hit Connie way below the belt. She glanced up at me and I saw her lip tremble. I put an arm around her and eased her into a deep leather chair. She kept her eyes down, staring at her hands in her lap.

Foster was looking at me coldly.

"We had a report from the F.B.I. through the Los Angeles office," he said. "Do you care to tell me your story?"

He asked as if he were fully prepared to disbelieve it, all or in part.

I went through the routine again, just as I had for the deputy in Westbrook, Indiana. I told it the same way I had then, but there was more to tell. I left out everything about Poole, the detective, only saying that after the F.B.I. man had appeared to accept Connie's identity tentatively, we had decided to come back to Los Angeles at once.

He listened in silence. I hoped I wouldn't have to tell the story anymore, because it was getting complicated and there were certain things involving myself that I didn't care to discuss.

When I had nearly finished, an intercom unit buzzed and Foster lifted the receiver to his ear.

"Very good," he said. "Ask them to come in."

The door opened and two men came in. They looked competent and official. Foster introduced them to us as local F.B.I. men. I braced myself, waiting for them to ask me why I'd kidnapped Connie myself, after pretending to be her protector.

But they didn't mention it. In fact, as the afternoon wore on, everybody paid less and less attention to me. All the concentration was on Connie. They weren't rough. They took it easy. But there were a lot of questions and several times I noticed them trying to trip her up. I noticed too that Connie was wearing down under it and I was about to interrupt when the F.B.I. agents stopped questioning her and said good-by to Foster. They were gone as suddenly as they had come.

Then Foster asked me to wait in the outer office for a while. I went out there and tried to look at a magazine, but the words kept blurring and I stared at the wall and waited. The secretary went in and out of her office with a shorthand notebook, made telephone calls, now and then stopped to ask me a question and finally disappeared. Connie came into the glass-walled office alone. She was in there for a few minutes, then returned to Foster's office. After a while she came out again and sat down beside me.

"He has to call Jeanie," Connie said.

I heard the receptionist dial a number, wait and ask for Jean Jordan. It took quite a while to get her on the line. Then it took much longer for Foster to talk to her, while Connie and I sat in the outer office, waiting. The secretary came out, dressed for the street and said goodnight to the receptionist and the stenographer. The receptionist began to polish her nails and look at her watch. The stenographer went on typing.

"Why does it take so long?" Connie said. "Why can't I talk to Jeanie?"

"Soon now," I said, patting her hand. "Try to hold on."

Finally Foster's door opened and he came over to us. He smiled professionally at both of us.

"Well, young lady," he said, "I imagine you'd like to see your sister."

"Oh, yes."

Connie jumped up. Foster frowned for a moment and I had a feeling we were just getting started. There were more hurdles to come, more channels.

"I've arranged for you to visit Miss Jean Jordan at eight o'clock this evening," he said. "I'm sorry that I will be unable to accompany you."

He glanced at me.

"I'll see that she gets there," I said.

He nodded.

"Thank you," he said. "That's all for now. I'll want to see you again tomorrow."

He held out his hand and Connie took it. Then he turned to his receptionist.

"Will you give the address of the Jordan home to Mr.—"

"Cross," I said.

"Mr. Cross."

The receptionist yawned and picked up a pencil. She wrote an address on a piece of scratch paper and handed it to me. I didn't recognize the street.

"It's in Bel Air," she said. "Go in the east entrance. Sunset Boulevard."

I thanked her and went back to Connie. Foster had already disappeared into his private office. We went outside and down to the car.

What a reception, I thought. A kid gets kidnapped, raped and mistreated for eight years, and when she comes home—nobody to meet her, no celebration, no nothing. Just a lot of questions in a lawyer's office and a handshake.

I tried to create our own private celebration with words, as I drove slowly through Beverly Hills, looking for a place we could eat and pay for it. But my words must have sounded forced because Connie remained quiet and listless. I asked, "What do you remember about Jeanie?"

She couldn't tell me anything specific. She wound up describing the way they had played together as children. Finally she gave up trying and said, "Jeanie is wonderful!"

I wondered how much of it was truly out of her memory and what part of it was something she had created in imagination during those long, dreary, painful years with Kretch and Madeleine. I wondered how close the real Jeanie would be to the image of Jeanie in Connie's mind.

Well, I thought, maybe before long we'll know. And maybe Jeanie is, after all, wonderful.

* * * *

After dinner, we got back in the car and I drove slowly, pretending it was hard to find the place, trying to kill time till eight o'clock, when Connie was to see Jean. She sat in silence, crowded against the door, her white face pressed against the window, staring out.

At five minutes to eight I turned into a long curving drive in Bel Air and headed for the front door of the Jordan mansion. Connie stared at it as we approached.

"Feel like home?" I asked.

"It's been so long," she said. "I think I remember, but it's been so long."

It was a wide, spacious house, Spanish style, with a red-tile roof. There was a dim light over a big bronze knocker on the front door. I lifted the knocker and let it fall, then lifted it again.

A Filipino in a white coat opened the door and peered out at us.

"Connie Jordan," I said to him, "to see her sister."

He mumbled something and closed the door. I felt like kicking it in, but I was too tired.

"Hang on, baby," I said. "It's almost over."

"Yes, Chris."

After a long time the door opened and the Filipino bobbed at us.

"Miss Jordan see you now," he said and backed away.

We walked through a wide entrance hall, through a high double door, ornately carved, into a gigantic living room, thickly carpeted, with Oriental throw rugs on top of the carpet. Connie gazed slowly around the room.

Her sister was waiting for us as we entered.

Meeting Jean Jordan was like coming up against the thin edge of a razor blade. Not that she was hard to look at. She was built the way we like to see them, full-bodied, not tall, not short. She wore an off-the-shoulder cocktail dress, sheer hose and red sandals with straps winding around her ankles and legs. She had blonde hair that hung halfway to her belt in the back and was banged across her forehead. The blondeness wasn't natural, but it was awfully well done. What I mean about the razor—her eyes and her manner were sharp; cold and sharp and hard.

She stood there, halfway across the big living room from us, with a highball glass in one hand, and if ever I've seen the exact opposite of sisterly affection, this was it. She just stood and looked us over and took a sip of her drink and pretty soon I said, "Miss Jordan?"

And she said, "Yes."

So we stood there a while longer and finally Connie took a few steps into the room and said, "Jeanie—you've changed your hair!"

Well, I thought, what else would you say at such a time? Maybe one thing was as good as another. Or as bad.

The blonde set her glass down on a coffee table and waited for Connie to walk up to her. Connie made it, stumblingly, flutteringly like a bird and put out her hands. The Jordan girl looked at her hands for a second, then took Connie's as though she were checking a table top for dust. They stood that way and looked at each other. I stayed where I was, near the door.

"Connie—?" the girl said.

She said it as if it were a bad word, though I guessed she knew most of the bad words and wouldn't hesitate to use them when appropriate.

"Don't you remember me, Jeanie?" Connie said.

"That's not the question," said the other girl. "The question is, what do you remember?"

Slowly Connie dropped her hands and backed away.

"Jeanie—aren't you glad to see me at all?"

The blonde shrugged and picked up her glass.

"It's not that," she said. "It's just that I'm not sure who I'm seeing."

Her voice was sharp, like the look in her eyes and the words came out hard and flat.

Well, I thought, it's a long time. Usually there's no love lost between sisters anyway—or brothers either for that matter. She'd have to have time to get used to it.

Connie was talking.

"I thought Mr. Foster told you—"

"Mr. Foster," said the blonde, "told me that you and some man were coming to see me." Her eyes caught mine over Connie's shoulder. I stared back at her. "Mr. Foster said you claimed to be Constance Jordan. That's all he said."

I moved over to join them.

"Thanks," I said. "I'll have a drink."

The blonde looked at me out of those hard eyes.

"Yes," she said slowly. "I guess you would, wouldn't you?"

I let it pass. She went to a cupboard and got out a bottle, a couple of glasses and a bottle of soda. There was a bell pull near the cupboard and she yanked on that and pretty soon the little Filipino came in with some ice. I guess he was psychic.

I made myself a stiff drink and looked at Connie.

"When I finish this," I said, "we'd better run along. Mr. Foster will take care of the details."

Connie stared at me. I don't know that she heard what I said. The blonde mixed herself a drink.

"There are some details Mr. Foster can't handle," she said. "Connie—your old room, and playroom are just as you left them. Wouldn't you like to go up there?"

"Yes," said Connie. "Now?"

"If you like."

There was something awfully phony about her sudden hospitality, but I couldn't figure out what it was. Connie glanced at me and at her, then looked off toward the stairs that went up along the far left side of the room. They were Spanish style, like the house, with a wrought-iron railing on the outside. Connie walked over to the steps, put one hand on the railing and turned to look back at us. I started after her and the blonde caught my arm.

"Not you," she said. "Just—Connie."

Then I got it. I didn't think I could match her steely glare, but I tried.

"Just running a little test?" I said.

She didn't answer.

"Listen," I said, "the kid's all beat up inside. You expect her to come back after eight years of sheer nightmare and have it just as if she'd never been gone? You expect her to be able to pick out her own room in a house like this after she's been sleeping for years on a straw tick in a goddam tent? What the hell are you—?"

"Shut up," she said.

Her well-developed bust was heaving a little. I saw she was more worked up than her face had shown.

"Did you ever have two million dollars?" she said to me between her teeth. "All your own? and a million girls trying to cut in on it? Did you ever open the door, day after day, for some ambitious little chit with some faked-up marks on her, with her hands out like this to take the money? Did you ever answer the telephone in the middle of the night and hear somebody say, 'Jeanie—this is Connie! Oh, my darling sister, how I've missed you!' Did you ever—?"

"All right," I said. "I'm sorry about your two million bucks."

But she wasn't through.

"And you," she said. "How much did you plan on yourself? What's your cut out of the deal?"

I looked at her for a long time.

"I could learn to hate you," I said.

She gave the look back—all of it.

"Then hate real good, Buster," she said. "Because I'm real tough. You have to be tough to be rich."

"I believe it."

"Shall we see how—Connie—is doing?"

Connie had disappeared up the stairs. The blonde set her glass down and walked over there. I followed her. Going up the stairs, my eyes were on a level with her buttocks and I watched them sway a little as she climbed. I was good and sore at her and I allowed myself to undress her mentally, without qualms. I almost plowed into her with my nose when she stopped suddenly and looked back and down at me. I raised my eyes and hers were cutting me open.

"There are ways to handle men like you," she grated, "and I know all of them."

"With all that money," I said, "it shouldn't be any trick for you. You could hire the entire Mafia if you had to."

"I wouldn't have to," she said.

We went on up to the top of the stairs.

There was a long corridor with rooms on both sides. All the doors were closed and they all looked alike to me. She'd probably had them all done alike on purpose, just to run this test. Your chances of picking one door—the right one—would be about one in twelve. A real long shot. Unless, of course, you really remembered. Still, a few of the ambitious fakers must have found the right one by accident. I wondered what tricks she had on the inside, after you found the door.

Connie was two-thirds of the way along the hall, moving slowly, glancing to both sides. Once she paused, held out a hand toward a door, then dropped her hand and went on. She went on to the last door on the right and then she stopped. The blonde stopped too and grabbed my arm again. Her long red fingernails bit into me through the cloth of my coat. We waited while Connie opened the door and looked inside. It seemed like a long time she stood there, and then slowly she walked in, leaving the door open.

When the blonde and I reached the open door, Connie was on her knees, running her hands over a small, battered rocking chair beside a Hollywood bed with a pink spread on it. The chair had a cane seat and back and the wood of the frame was old and faded, with dark stains here and there. The room wasn't large. It was a corner room and there were windows on two sides than ran into the corner opposite the door to the hall where the blonde and I stood. There was a high chiffonier to our right and a tinted photograph in a chrome frame. The girl in the photograph looked like she might have been the blonde, Jean, only her hair was dark, like Connie's, and wrapped in braids around her head. The Hollywood bed was in the corner under the windows and the rocking chair was at the foot of the bed. There was a bookcase on the wall opposite the bed, still filled with books with bright colored bindings, and beside the bookcase another door stood slightly ajar.

"It's been changed," Connie was say. "The chair used to be by the bookcase."

I glanced at the blonde, but she was staring down at Connie, her breast heaving again, as I had seen it downstairs. Connie looked up at us. Her hand indicated the open door.

"The playroom—is in there," she said.

The blonde and I watched as she got to her feet and crossed the room to the playroom door, opened it wide and walked in. Then we followed her. The light was dim, but not too dim for seeing. The air was stale and a little musty, as if the room had been closed for a long time.

There was a jumble of furniture, mostly children's things, a table with four chairs, a small overstuffed wing chair with a chintz cover, a junior-sized ironing board with a real iron on it, a play stove and refrigerator. Against the wall were boxes with toys piled in them; dolls, teddy bears, tops, balls—everything kids would want to play with. In one corner was a desk with pigeonholes stuffed with papers, crayons and odds and ends.

Connie had knelt beside one of the toy boxes and was rummaging through it. Her hands moved faster and faster, as if she were looking for something special and not finding it. The blonde beside me watched her closely. Her breasts weren't heaving now and I wondered whether she was holding her breath.

Suddenly Connie's hands stopped moving. Her face turned to the blonde's face and light seemed to be coming out of her eyes.

"The monkey puppet!" she said. "It's gone. Where is it, Jeanie? Where's the monkey?"

There was a period of silence. The blonde had slumped, as if someone had struck her. She leaned against the door jamb, her hands at her sides and her eyes were closed. Somewhere deep in the house I heard the tinkle of a bell. Must be the doorbell, I thought.

"Where's the monkey, Jeanie?" Connie said again. "Please—" Still the blonde didn't move or speak. I looked at her.

"All right," I said quietly. "Where is it?"

She didn't look at me. She pushed herself away from the door and moved across the room to the desk in the corner. She reached into it and her hand came out with something that she handed to Connie, still on her knees beside the toy box.

It was one of those children's puppets of cloth—a monkey's head and arms that you pulled on over your hand and made it move with your fingers. Thousands of them all over the country. But this was a particular one in a particular room—and Connie had remembered it.

She pulled it onto her hand and played with it, making the weird head bob and nod this way and that, making the two paws clap together.

"Monkey, monkey, bottle of beer—" she said slowly, then looked up, smiling, at the blonde. "Remember, Jeanie?"

The blonde remembered all right, but she didn't say so. She turned and walked to the door, went past me blindly and I heard her going away down the hall toward the stairs.

Yes, sister, I thought, have another drink. A million-dollar drink. On the house.

Time stood still—maybe went backward—while Connie knelt on the floor, playing with the monkey, rubbing, it now and then across her cheek, wiggling the paws and head, repeating over and over her childhood rhyme, "Monkey, monkey, bottle of beer…"

After a while I leaned over and touched her shoulder. She looked up at me.

"We'd better go call Mr. Foster," I said. "Then I guess you could come back later, to stay, if you want to. But it's not official yet."

"You mean Mr. Foster has to say I'm really who I am?"

"Not just Mr. Foster. A lot of people. But I think we'd better call him right away."

This hunch had been growing stronger in me every minute.

Connie got up and came with me into the hall.

"Where did Jeanie go?" she said.

"Downstairs," I said. "I think the doorbell rang."

We went to the head of the stairs and Connie held onto my arm as we went down. The light had been turned on in the living room, soft, indirect lights that splashed a gentle glow on the ceiling and over the walls. The blonde was sitting with a man on the love seat in front of the coffee table. They both had highballs and I was plenty thirsty.

When we reached the bottom of the steps, Jean got up and walked over to us.

"We'll run along," I said. "Thanks for the drink."

Her eyes were flat and gray, no longer sharp and hard, but lifeless. She nodded toward Connie.

"She might as well stay, if she wants to," she said.

I took Connie's arm and headed for the door.

"Maybe she can come back later," I said.

The guy who had been sitting with Jean got up and turned around to look at us. The lights were low, but it wasn't hard to recognize him—the dark eyes, the faint scar beside his nose, the big hands, the wide shoulders. My good pal, Roger Poole.

I hurried Connie to the door. She held back, looking over her shoulder at Jean, but I made her come with me. I had strong feelings about it. Very strong.

"Good night," I said hurriedly. "We'll get in touch with you."

I bundled Connie through the door, pulling it to behind me, and we went down to the borrowed car on the drive. I jammed it into gear and twisted the wheel to follow the faint gray curb. I couldn't get away from there fast enough.

"Chris," Connie said, "why do we have to go away so fast?"

"I'll try to tell you later," I said. "I don't know whether I ever can."

CHAPTER 12

I cruised for a while, trying to figure out a place to go. I still didn't know how Poole fitted in, but I now knew he didn't always work alone and I knew I didn't want him coming around in the night, pounding on the door.

I would have to return Doc Brockman's car. I had about twenty-five dollars left and if Connie and I had to hole up for any length of time, that would go in a hurry. I had no idea how long it would take to go through the red tape she would have to go through.

I finally settled on a small hotel I remembered on Cahuenga Boulevard, just off Hollywood. It was dark, on the run-down side, with a row of second-story windows fronting on the street and a bath at the end of the hall. We could get a room there for a buck and a half a day.

Inside, I paid for a couple of days in advance and we went up to a boxlike room in which the bed took up most of the space. I left Connie there, locking the door as I went out, and walked to the end of the hall where there was a public phone fastened to the wall. I found Foster's name and residence in the Western Section of the directory. He lived out in Beverly Hills. I got his home and it took a while for him to get to the phone.

He remembered me after a minute and said, "Yes, Cross. What is it?"

I told him what had happened out at the big house in Bel Air, how Connie had found her old room and asked about the monkey. When I finished there was a pause. Then he said, "Where is the young lady now?"

"With me."

"Didn't Miss Jordan ask her to stay?"

"She said she could if she wanted to. She wasn't very cordial about it."

"The girl didn't want to stay?"

"I think she did."

Another pause.

"Then why didn't she?"

"I wouldn't let her."

"And why not?"

"I had a hunch she might not be safe there."

"Not safe! Are you crazy?"

"Maybe. But that was my hunch."

"Look here, Cross," he said, and his voice had acquired a new tone—of threat and warning. "You seem to be taking a lot on your shoulders. You're not entirely clean in this business. I advise you to watch your step."

"I'll take care of myself," I said. "But who's going to take care of Connie?"

There was quite a long pause.

"If the young lady will come to my office in the morning," he said then, "we'll get to work on the red tape."

"How long will it take?"

"I don't know."

"What time in the morning?"

"Nine-thirty."

"I'll see she's there."

"Be sure that you do."

He hung up.

I stood there for a minute, wondering about him. I couldn't figure it out, the whole play since we'd got back to town. Here was Connie Jordan, heiress, returned after eight years of mystery. This was big—important—good for a banner headline any day of the week. Yet, we had been back for more than twenty-four hours and there hadn't been a line in any of the papers.

And here was I, a nobody, a bum, not in the same league with Connie or Jean or Foster at all. I was wanted for so-called rape in Ohio. I had practically forced Connie to travel with me clear across the country. For all they could know, I might take her away again. But I was still on the loose.

When would they lower the boom?

I was still wondering as I left the phone and went back to the room.

Connie was standing by the window, looking into the street. Her dark hair hung around her shoulders and I noticed the sheen it had now. When I'd first seen her, it had been dead-looking, dull. She'd filled out some too and the cheap dress she'd bought that first day was a little tight here and there. I pictured her a few weeks from now, healthy again, dolled up in new expensive clothes, with a little makeup on her face—she'd be a beautiful girl.

Whose? I wondered. Whose beautiful girl would she be?

When she turned from the window, I saw she'd been crying.

"Chris," she said, "Jeanie wasn't glad to see me."

My stomach knotted.

"Oh, well—" I started.

"Why, Chris? I was glad to see her."

"I guess it's hard for her to get used to it, because it's been so long."

"We used to have fun together."

"Sure, honey."

"I was—almost afraid of her."

"Let's take the car back to the doctor," I said.

I wanted to get her off this subject. I didn't know how to handle it.

On the way to where I had parked the car, we passed a liquor store and I pushed myself on by. I noticed I didn't have to push so hard as I would have a month before. A month before I couldn't have passed it at all.

* * * *

I had hoped we could put Doc's car in the garage and get away. I'd hoped he would have company, or be tied up some way. But when I went to the door to return the keys, Doc opened it himself and held it wide.

"Come in, Chris," he said.

"We can't stay," I said, taking Connie's arm and leading her into the living room.

"You can stay enough to play thirty-two bars of something," he said.

I introduced them.

"Connie Jordan," I said, "Doctor Brockman."

At the name Jordan, Doc flicked his eyes at me, then looked at Connie again and smiled. He was a handsome guy, tall, with dark skin and hair and large, clear eyes that could look you over before you knew what was going on. I'd asked him once whether any of his female patients ever fell in love with him.

"They all do," he'd said. "But they would fall in love with me if I looked like Gargantua. It's the relationship—not the appearance."

I saw him study Connie and knew he had registered something on the name Jordan. But he didn't say anything about it. He was very gentle with her. I noticed that he studied her most of the time, as we sat down in the big living room. I wondered what he was thinking, but I couldn't very well ask.

The concert grand, a beautiful ebony piano, was across from me with a light behind it. I sat and looked at it for a while and then, because I couldn't help myself, I got up and went over to it. I had played it many times. It was an instrument that produced great tone almost automatically. But the way I was feeling, with the worry about Connie biting at the edges of my mind, I thought I would probably destroy the tone before it could get started. Still, I couldn't keep my fingers off the keys.

I played a couple of new tunes, improvising the arrangements, and they didn't come out too well. I tackled a Gershwin Prelude that I remembered Doc had liked in the old days, but I missed too many of the notes. I couldn't get an even tone and altogether I made hash out of it. I decided I'd only been fooling myself back there on the road, when I'd told Connie I thought I could play again.

I quit finally. I noticed there was a bright light near Connie's chair and she kept blinking, as if trying to get away from it. She seemed listless and groggy and I wondered why Doc didn't turn the lamp off. He was sitting in half-light himself in a deep leather chair. I got up from the piano, walked over to where Connie was sitting and switched off the lamp.

This seemed to startle Doc, who got up then and thanked me for playing—without congratulations—and said, "I imagine you'd like a drink. Miss Jordan?"

"She doesn't take it," I said for her.

Doc looked at me, turned toward the kitchen, stopped and looked at me again. I excused myself to Connie and followed him to the kitchen, where he got down a bottle of good bourbon, a couple of glasses and some ice and made us a couple of drinks.

He didn't say anything for quite a while, then he looked at me out of those wise eyes and said, "The girl is sick, Chris. Is she the lost heiress to the Jordan millions?"

"Yes, she is. How sick?" I asked.

"Pretty sick. Her eyes—Excuse me for diagnosing your date's condition."

I thought about it for a minute and said, "It's a long story. I don't have time to tell you now."

"All right," he said. "Whenever you feel like it. Is this big enough for you?"

He held up one of the glasses.

"I should have stopped you," I said. "I haven't been taking much the last few days."

He looked at me sharply.

"How does it feel?"

"Good," I said. "So far."

He poured the whisky down the sink.

"Glass of orange juice?" he said.

"That would be fine."

He went to the refrigerator. I could smell the liquor he'd thrown out and I saw what he had poured in his own glass and I had to hold very tight while he found some orange juice in the box and poured it for me.

When he handed it to me, along with another for Connie, his face was serious.

"It doesn't feel so good right now, does it?" he said.

"No, Doc."

"I don't want any either," he said and poured his own drink out.

"You're wasting a hell of a lot of good whisky," I said.

"Yes," he said. "We'll never miss it. Maybe."

"You were saying, about the girl—"

"We'd better get back to her," he said. "I shouldn't have spoken about it. Forget it."

"I can't forget it."

After a moment he said, "I'm sorry, Chris."

In the living room Connie still sat in the same position, watching us, her eyes flat, her hands restless in her lap. We drank the orange juice quickly and I went to help her up. She came along without question.

I found myself under new tension. I wished the Doc hadn't said anything. But in another way, if something had to be said, maybe this was the time for it. I wanted to talk to him about it, but I had to take care of Connie first. I thought maybe I could call him at his office the next day.

But I couldn't afford to call him.

Doc offered to drive us home, but I told him where we were staying and that the bus would take us within half a block and he let us go. He took Connie's hand as we started out and smiled at her warmly.

"I hope you'll come back some time, with Chris," he said.

"Maybe," she said and pulled her hand away.

She's had enough, I thought. Maybe too much.

We walked up to the corner and waited for the bus at Crenshaw. Connie didn't say anything at all. We had to wait quite a while and by the time we got back to the hotel it was after midnight.

We undressed in the dark, as usual, and crawled in on opposite sides of the bed. I hadn't touched Connie in bed since that first night in Westbrook, Indiana, but we'd had to sleep together for reasons of economy. For the same reasons, neither of us had anything like pajamas or nightgowns. Sometimes it had been hard to leave her alone. But tonight I was tired and went right to sleep.

It must have been around four in the morning when I woke and knew she wasn't in bed with me. I was scared at first and sat up straight, trying to find her and get conscious both at the same time. Then there was a small sound and I turned my head and saw her standing by the window. There was a thin, gauzelike curtain over the window and the dull glow from the street highlighted her slim, pale body, softened the contours so that her breasts seemed not quite as large as they really were and the rest of her looked fuller and rounder than in full light.

"Can't sleep, Connie?" I asked.

She turned, startled, to look at me.

"Sorry," I said and climbed off the bed.

It was a close, muggy night and no breeze came through the window. The curtain hung still except when one or the other of us touched it.

She turned her face to me and I saw there were tears on it again.

"You ought to get some sleep," I said. "Long day tomorrow."

After a while she said, "Chris—it doesn't seem as if I've come home. It seems all wrong."

"It will be all right in a couple of days. Mr. Foster—"

"It's Jeanie. She didn't want me to come home—did she, Chris? She hoped I'd never come home."

"No, it's just that—"

"And that Mr. Poole—the one that was with her tonight. He wasn't going to bring me home, was he, Chris?"

I kept quiet.

"It was you that brought me home. And now I don't want to be home. If Jeanie hates me, it won't be any good at home."

She reached out and put her hand on my chest. It was the first time she had ever touched my body of her own accord, except to push me away. Her hand was small and warm and the fingers were trembling.

"I don't want to go home, Chris," she said. "I don't care about the money. I just want to stay with you."

I tried to laugh.

"In a place like this?" I said.

"It wouldn't always be a place like this. You could get a job."

"That's just the way you feel tonight," I said. "You can say now you don't care about the money, but someday you'll wish you had it. It belongs to you, Connie. Your father wanted it to be yours."

She looked at my face and her fingers twisted the flesh of my chest.

"You don't have to live with Jean," I said. "You can have your own place, anywhere you want it."

She seemed a little startled. I guess she hadn't even thought of her own place. The big house in Bel Air was home as she had left it and I guess she figured that was where she had to go.

"But I couldn't live all by myself," she said.

"I'll stick around, Connie, till it's all straightened out. It's been rough for you and you're upset. But it will all level off and be all right."

Her fingers were still working at my chest, twisting, prodding, stroking as her dark eyes searched my face through the dim light. She put her other hand on me and stood close. Inside me somewhere a small knot of excitement gathered, began to grow, a feeling I had fought against for days.

"Chris," she whispered, "if I was really your wife—what would it be like then?"

"Listen honey—" But the only listening she was doing was with her hands. They moved slowly at first, then faster, feverishly, touching me and drawing back, as if she were frightened and returning again. I didn't know how to handle her, she was like a bird, half-bold, half-frightened, approaching and backing off again. I stroked her gently, trying clumsily to speak to her with my hands. I put my arms around her and she came against me and we kissed, a long, soft kiss. She relaxed for a moment, then stiffened and pushed away and ran to the bed.

I stood by the window, afraid to move. The memory of how it had been before, that first time in Indiana, held me back. I couldn't take the chance of putting that fear back in her. I couldn't stand it for her and I couldn't stand it for myself.

I remember glancing out the window, and across the street was a wide, dark store window with a big lighted sign in front reading: pianos—for sale or rent. I remembered the place. I remembered a beautiful concert grand they'd had in there a few years back and it rented for forty dollars a month. I stood there by the window, thinking about it, and I wished I could get the keyboard under my fingers again. I wanted to work this thing out of me before Connie had a chance to build it up and turn it down again. I wanted to pound and smash on the keyboard till the music drowned what I was feeling.

She called to me softly in the dark across the room and I turned. She was kneeling on the bed, watching me. Her dark hair was tumbled around her white face and her breasts were pale and darkly tipped and beautiful.

"Chris—" she said again.

I walked slowly to the bed and sat down on its edge. She gave me her small searching hands. For a moment then I was the one to draw back. Pictures flashed through my mind—the years and years for her on a straw tick in a tent and the men, one after the other, thoughtless, careless, rough, hasty, using her secretly and hurrying away in the night. And I thought, No! I can't be just another one of them.

Then I felt her hands on me, unsure, questioning, and when I touched her now she trembled and I knew that this was new for her and for me too. It was like the first time for both of us, fresh and clean and right. I remember thinking, It's true then. You can shake those chains that tie you to the past. No matter what it's been before, it can start over. It can be like a new life—as if you were a different person.

And then I didn't think any longer, because there was Connie and the night and her warm, young, new body. And the chains snapped, as if we had been on a raft on the river, tied up, then suddenly set free. We drifted down the river that grew, wider and wider, tossed a little this way and that at first, then striking the swift main current and going with it faster and faster and then we became part of the river itself and I heard the music...

CHAPTER 13

I got Connie to Foster's office at nine-thirty in the morning. Foster was still cold, but made no threats. Connie seemed more relaxed. I told her I would come back for her at four-thirty in the afternoon. Foster said nothing to me when I left.

I caught a streetcar from Beverly Hills back to Hollywood. It was a fine day, with sunshine, and the smog not too thick. It felt good to stand on the street and watch people walk past the corner of Hollywood and Vine. I thought for a while about what Doc had said about Connie being sick, but when I remembered how it had been after we'd got back to the hotel, and when I thought how Foster had at least kept his mouth shut, most of the worry faded away. It was bound to come out all right. We couldn't have made the long trip for nothing.

I walked down to the union building on Vine Street and went through the red tape of getting myself reinstated. They told me what I knew—that I couldn't take any work at all for three months, and then I could take casuals. I didn't recognize anybody working there in the office and nobody recognized me either. But even if we'd all been close friends, it wouldn't have made any difference.

After I got through with that I walked back up Vine Street and stood around for a while outside Coffee Dan's and ran into three or four people I knew. We didn't celebrate any old home week. Business was way off in town and that's what we talked about. I began to figure out that it didn't make much difference whether I could work or not. There wouldn't be any work to do. But I didn't worry. There would be work at the aircraft plants, and it would pay enough so that I could rent a piano and practice, and when the three months had passed, I'd be ready. And there would be Connie...

I felt good, full of sunshine and the memory of the night before. I felt so good I got cocky. There was a small bar up the street and I went and stood outside, looking at it, and then I walked past it, slowly, half a dozen times, thumbing my nose at it each time I passed the door. Finally I went inside and sat down on one of the stools. I still had about twenty dollars left in my pocket and I ordered a shot of whisky and a bottle of beer. The bartender brought them and I paid him. I sat there for a long time, looking at the shot, smelling it, lifting it and passing it back and forth under my nose. Then I put it down carefully without spilling it, got off the stool and headed for the door. The bartender called after me.

"What's the matter? Something wrong with it?"

I laughed at him.

"Who needs it?" I said.

The bartender shook his head sadly and I went on out. I had lunch at Coffee Dan's and got another paper. When I finished that I walked over to Cahuenga and up toward the hotel. At the piano store I stopped and looked in the window for a while. The big concert grand I remembered was gone, but they had some good-looking Steinways of various sizes. I went inside and it was cool and dark in there.

There were no customers and the girl at the desk in the back of the room offered to help me and when I said I was just browsing around, she left me alone. I found an instrument with a good tone and improvised for a while on it and then settled down and tried to play something. It didn't sound very good. I told the girl I'd quit if it bothered her but she asked me please to go right ahead.

I ran a few scales and arpeggios, trying to get loosened up and then tackled some Ravel and Debussy that I remembered. I hit most of the notes all right, but I couldn't produce any tone. It was ragged and uneven and half the time at least it was just plain dead. I worked myself into quite a sweat and then changed to another piano and fooled around for a while. I managed to relax again and pretty soon I went back to the first instrument and began to play a Chopin Berceuse. It was in D-flat Major and it was all tone. Its whole effect depended on a long sustained, legato tone. The only guy I had ever heard who could really play it was Brailowsky and he made some of those simple runs in it sound like flowing water. Without that tone, it sounded like absolutely nothing.

It sounded like nothing the way I played it, at first. About a third of the way along there are some descending thirds that run down very fast and very piano, winding up with a trill, and the whole passage sounds like the beating of small birds' wings. Then a few measures later, the thing repeats, more or less, only now the thirds are broken and the fluttering sound is intensified. I stumbled along through it, wishing I could cut the sound down to where it ought to be and still hit all those notes, and I got to thinking of Connie. I thought of her hands, the way they had felt on my body the night before. I remembered her breath, quick and soft against my face, caught and released again, her breath in my ears, on my throat. And suddenly, near the end of the Berceuse, I heard it—the tone, the sound I had to make in order to make music, the strange, projected sound that is the difference between true music and just another collection of notes arranged on a mathematical scale.

It didn't last long—only a few bars, and I lost it again before I finished. But I had heard it once and my hands had been relaxed and I knew I could do it again. I knew it would come back. I knew I wasn't finished.

I sat for a long time, staring at the keyboard, and when I looked up at a clock, it was time to go for Connie. As I walked out into the street, I felt as if I were holding something in my hands, something I could give to Connie, the way I had given her the job in the Blackstone Hotel back in Indiana. Only this new thing was so much bigger. This was a real big thing. I wondered when she could ever know how big it was.

It was a ten-minute walk from the bus depot to Foster's office and I took it easy, enjoying the afternoon sun and the bright, clean, well-run look of Beverly Hills. When I reached Foster's building I was still a few minutes early and I walked up the stairs to the second floor and down the hall to his office. The receptionist asked me to wait a minute and I sat down. Connie was nowhere in sight. I waited about five minutes and the girl said I could go in.

Connie wasn't in Foster's private office either. Foster was there, seated behind his big desk, and beside him, a little off to one side and back, sat Roger Poole. The two of them looked up at me when I walked in. Foster started to flash his professional smile, then cut it off and indicated a chair facing the desk. Poole's face didn't move at all. It was the first really good, full-face look I'd got at him since Indiana. The white scar was quite noticeable. I sat down and looked at Foster.

"Where's Connie?" I asked.

"She went home," he said.

"With her sister?"

"That's right."

"She wouldn't do that," I said.

He blinked. He had bushy gray brows and they twitched up and down.

"And why not?" he said. "What would be more natural?"

"Why did you let her go?"

"Now take it easy, Cross." He swung his hand toward the other one. "This is Mr. Poole."

"I've met Mr. Poole," I said.

Poole said nothing.

"Miss Jean Jordan sent Mr. Poole to Westbrook, Indiana, to assist Connie, after they talked on the telephone."

"All right," I said.

"But you seemed to have other ideas," Foster said. "Possibly you thought you could handle the situation better than Poole."

I glanced at Poole. He glanced at me, idly, without interest.

"O.K.," I said. "Maybe I made a mistake."

Foster pressed the point.

"I would be interested to know what made you do it. Why did you refuse to co-operate with Poole?"

I shrugged.

"Just a hunch," I said. "I would be interested to know why Connie decided to go home, without letting me know."

"As I said, it seems natural enough to me."

"She wouldn't have done it," I said stubbornly. "She wouldn't have just walked away without leaving word."

Foster went a little stuffy.

"Do you think I'm lying to you"?

"I don't say that. I just ask questions. Why did she go? Who handled it? Was her sister here?"

Foster's voice sounded as if he were trying to keep himself under control. He did pretty well at it.

"Try to understand, Cross. Constance has suffered intolerably for many years. She was virtually a child when she was torn from her family and subjected to—unspeakable experiences."

"Go on," I said. "I'm with it."

"Naturally she needs the love and care of her own sister. She needs rest and seclusion. Today in the office here, she broke down, rather badly. Her sister feels she may have a nervous breakdown—or worse."

"Worse?"

"The experiences Constance has gone through could unbalance the healthiest mind."

"She was all right last night."

He gave me the big-brow treatment.

"Are you a doctor, Cross?"

"Goddam it—!"

And then I stopped. Because I was not a doctor. And because it happened I'd talked to a doctor the night before who had said something like what Foster was saying now. I began to feel sick myself.

I got up from the chair and faced him across the desk. "Maybe you're on the level," I said. "Maybe you're doing what you think is right. But me, I've got to find out for myself. I've got to see Connie."

I headed for the door. I don't know how he did it, but by the time I reached it, Poole was standing between it and me. He didn't move toward me. He just stood there, leaning nonchalantly against the door.

"Cross!" Foster said sharply.

I looked back at him and listened again to his rich, dramatic voice.

"There's something more," he said and he sounded almost human. "Both of the Jordan girls are grateful to you."

"It was nothing."

"They wanted to show their appreciation in some substantial way. They asked me to give you this."

He reached into a drawer, tossed a large white envelope onto the desk. I walked back there and picked it up. I opened it and looked inside. There was a check. It was a check for five thousand dollars, made out to Christopher Cross, signed by Foster, *"for Constance Jordan."*

So already they were signing her own checks for her.

Foster looked at his watch. I stuck the check back in the envelope and dropped it on the desk.

"No thanks," I said.

He blinked those brows at me.

"It's not chicken feed," he said.

"I don't know," I said. "Maybe after last night it looks like chicken feed to me."

Foster ran his hands carefully through his thick hair.

"You ought to know," he said, "that I spent considerable time convincing the F.B.I. that you were helping us when you brought Connie back from Indiana on your own initiative. They were inclined to look on it as kidnapping. I refrained from telling them you were wanted in Ohio on a charge of rape."

I looked at Poole. His face was impassive.

"So you and that big ape got together," I said.

"You did quite a job on him," Poole said softly. "I had a hard time bringing him around."

"I didn't rape anybody," I said.

Poole shrugged. Foster was talking again.

"I don't know," he said, "how long I can protect you from your own past. I am prepared to try, if you will cooperate."

"Cooperate?" I said stupidly. "By staying away from Connie Jordan? Is that it?"

"That's part of it," he said, "and by restraining any impulses you may have to talk about her return, especially to newspaper reporters."

"How much do I owe you for legal assistance?"

"Not a cent. I did it for Jean and Constance as much as for you."

"You're very generous. I'd like to speak to Connie on the telephone. Maybe I could do it here."

He hesitated for a second, then rubbed his brows wearily with his fingers.

"You don't seem to understand, Cross," he said. "It is the feeling of everyone concerned that it will be best for Connie to have no contact with you until she has a chance to rest and regain some of her strength."

"That's Connie's feeling too?" I said.

"Yes."

"I don't believe it," I said.

He sighed and shifted in his chair. He pulled open a deep drawer at one side of the desk. I saw there was a tape recorder in it.

"I'm sorry," he said, after he'd switched it on. "I'd hoped we wouldn't have to go this far. I'm going to play a part of the conversation among Jean Jordan, Constance and myself, when we were discussing where Connie ought to go."

The tape rustled across the top of the recorder and gradually the volume increased. The first voice I heard was clearly Foster's.

(…I think that's all for today," he said. "Constance seems tired."

"She's awfully tired—and upset. Aren't you Connie?" That was the blonde, Jean Jordan, talking.

"Yes, Jean," said another voice. It was Connie. Certainly it was Connie's voice. I tried to tell myself it was somebody else's, but it wouldn't work. It was a good recorder and I knew Connie's voice.

"Don't you think you ought to come home and rest now?" said Jean.

"I don't know…" Connie said, her voice weak.

Foster cut into the conversation again.

"Tell us what you want to do, Constance. Do you want to go back to the hotel in Hollywood, with Chris? Or do you want to go home with Jean?"

There was a slight pause on the tape and then Connie's voice said again, clearly and unmistakably, "I want to go home with Jean."

Foster switched the thing off and closed the drawer. I stared at where the recorder had been, hearing it over and over in my head as if she were still repeating it, here in this quiet room.

"I want to go home with Jean."

I couldn't think of anything to say. I turned and headed for the door. I couldn't figure it out—even now. I didn't understand the play at all.

But I had understood the words on the tape recorder and I had understood that it was Connie speaking and the meaning of what she had said was quite clear.

I got to the door and Poole opened it for me. I didn't look at him, but I heard what he said, quietly and firmly as I passed.

"Don't try to hide, Cross. It won't do any good."

I went past him, out of the office, downstairs and into the street.

I walked up the street to a small tavern and hit a kind of jackpot. There was a happy drunk in the place, setting them up for everybody. I don't know where he had got it, but he was flinging money in all directions. I accepted straight shots with beer to chase them, and in half an hour I was relaxed. Also, I had money left in my pocket.

It was dark when I left the tavern and I walked to the Beverly Hills station and sat on a bench. One of the big busses came in from Santa Monica, heading for downtown L.A. and I watched the passengers changing. I didn't think about anything. I had drunk enough to do some forgetting and there wasn't anything ahead to think about. I knew it would take a long time to forget everything that needed forgetting, but I knew it could be done. I'd done it before. I got on a bus and headed for my hotel so I could start doing it in comfort. Between the bus and the hotel I picked up a couple of bottles.

For four days I didn't leave my room except to go to the bathroom and, now and then, to a joint on the corner for a sandwich. I slept much of the time and the two bottles held out. Eventually, every sleeping period wound up with a nightmare that would waken me and I'd have two or three quick shots and maybe go out in the sun to get warm and after a while I could get to sleep again.

There was a battered blonde living in the room next to mine. I would meet her sometimes going to and from the bathroom. I wasn't interested in her, but I noticed a couple of times she walked unsteadily and it gave me a sense of companionship. She went in and out irregularly, as I did and I wondered whether we were both doing the same thing, she with her stock and I with mine. I wondered how much stock she had on hand. The time would come when mine would run out. Then I wondered whether she was wondering the same things about me. We never spoke to each other, but a couple of times we bumped into each other in the hall. At these times we would both murmur, "Excuse me," step carefully around each other and go our separate ways; round and round the circle—down the hall, back to the room, into bed, down the hall, endlessly, hour after hour.

Aside from the nightmares, I felt secure and untouchable, because I had the stock right in my room and almost ten dollars in cash against the day when the liquor would run out.

I had one or two dreams about Connie, but they never lasted long and I never thought about her when I was awake. One of the dreams was quite realistic and I woke from it in a sweat. I'd seen Connie in a magnificent bed and then I had seen the scar-faced detective open the door and walk toward the bed with a knife in his hand. I tried to scream at

Connie to waken her, but I couldn't make any sound and I woke myself, terrified and gasping.

Afterward I lay still in bed for a long time and tried to force myself to get up and call to make sure Connie was all right. But I didn't make it. I thought of everything they had on me and of what Foster had said about his talk with the F.B.I. And most of all I thought about the voices on the tape that he had run through his machine for me. I had been dismissed and paid off, in Connie's voice and with Connie's money. So the hell with it. The bloody hell with it now and forever and please pass the bottle, which was so conveniently located beside my bed.

CHAPTER 14

The blonde knocked on my door sometime in the morning of the third day. I was sitting up in bed, looking at a paper. There was a bottle, two-thirds full, on a chair beside the bed and I tightened the cap and stuffed it under the bedclothes to hide it.

"Come in," I said.

She came in. She was wearing a faded chenille bathrobe, once pink, gathered around her loosely. She wasn't a bad-looking girl, but she hadn't bothered to take much care of herself recently and her hair and face showed it. There was an unlighted cigarette hanging from her mouth. She closed the door and leaned against it, spoke around her cigarette.

"I need a match," she said.

"I can't get out of bed," I said, "because I've got nothing on below the waist. I think there's a match in my coat pocket."

The coat was hanging over a chair at the foot of the bed. She walked over there and found a pack of matches, lit her cigarette and sat down on the chair, staring out the window.

"How're you coming?" she asked.

"Hmn?"

After a while she shrugged.

"Oh, well," she said, "I thought as long as we were neighbors, we might as well be—neighborly. We could tell each other our life stories."

She coughed and drew her robe tighter across her breasts. If she was waiting for me to offer her a drink, she would wait a long time. The stuff in the bottle was liquid gold. But she didn't need a drink. She went ahead and told me the story of her life without it.

It was a long story. I dozed off several times and I got awfully thirsty, but I was afraid to pull out the bottle for fear she would want to help me drink it. Finally in one of the dozes I had another bad dream about Connie and woke up yelling, struggling to get out of bed.

When I got clear awake, I saw that the blonde had retreated to the door and was standing rigid against it, staring at me. I got back into bed and covered myself up. I had knocked the bottle off into the floor and I groped with one hand till I found it. When I set it on the chair beside the bed, my hand was shaking.

"What happened?" the blonde said. "You got the D.T.'s?"

"No," I said. "Sit down. Relax. I've got a story too."

She started to open the door.

"I better go home," she said.

I didn't want her to leave.

"No!" I said. I held out the bottle. "Here. Have a drink. Sit down. I got to tell you this. It's my turn."

She didn't really want to stay, but the bottle drew her. There was an extra glass on the dresser and she carried it to the bed. I poured a generous shot into it and she sat down again in the chair at the foot of the bed.

"See," I said, "there was this chick I picked up…"

And I told her. The whole thing, all of it, the words tumbling out like peanuts out of a sack. I could hardly wait to get it out. And when I finished, I was exhausted, as if I had just given a concert or played six sets of tennis.

The blonde didn't say anything. She finished her drink, carried the glass to the dresser and started edging toward the door.

"You don't believe it," I said.

She shrugged. She got the door open and stood with her hand on the knob.

"I don't say I don't believe it," she said. "But if it's true, why don't you call up the papers and give 'em the story? Smoke 'em out."

"Huh!" I said.

"It's up to you," she said. "The papers will give you protection—if you need it."

I was very serious.

"Maybe so," I said. "It's a big deal."

Then all of a sudden I had to laugh. "Big deal." Here we were, two lushes in a cheap hotel, stoned to the eyeballs, talking over a big deal. Between us, we'd be lucky to raise twenty bucks. I rolled on the bed laughing and pretty soon I heard the blonde go out, slamming the door as she went. I laughed some more and had another drink and after a while I passed out.

But when I woke again, in the middle of the afternoon, I began to think about it, about calling the papers.

Why not? I thought. Maybe I could sell them the story, pick up a little loose change.

I went out and got a sandwich and when I got back to the hotel I felt pretty cocky. The telephone seemed to stare at me from the end of the hall and I walked back there and thumbed a battered directory till I found the number of one of the local tabloids. I dialed the number and asked for the city editor. When I told him I had an exclusive story for him, he said, "Wait a minute," and pretty soon another guy came on.

"Yeah? Go ahead," he said. He sounded bored.

I told him I'd brought the Jordan girl back home.

"Who?" he said.

"Connie Jordan. Been missing eight years—"

"O.K.," he said, "go ahead. Who are you?"

"It doesn't matter," I said.

I felt myself weaving a little and I began to have a cagey feeling. How did I know but what the reporter was Poole's brother or something?

"Constance Jordan," I said. "The kidnapped heiress. Look into it."

I hung up. I was shaking again. I leaned against the wall under the telephone and waited for the shakes to let up. The blonde came out of the bathroom, saw me and stopped.

"How did it go?" she said.

"It stank," I said. "It was a stinking idea in the first place."

"So I'm sorry," she said and went to her room.

After a long time I made it back to my own room and flopped onto the bed. I started to cry. Trying to stop it brought on the shakes again and I managed to find the bottle and drink myself to sleep—a long, deep, black sleep.

Late in the afternoon of the next day, I woke and when I held my hands out in front of me, they weren't shaking. I felt relaxed, but weak and used up. I rolled out of bed onto my knees, then pushed against the bed to get on my feet.

In the bathroom I filled the tub with hot water and got in and soaked myself and cleaned up. I had found a razor with a dull blade and managed to shave myself. My clothes were wrinkled and dirty, but I shook them out and I knew they would get by for a while. I didn't plan to go far. My bottle had one good shot left in it, but I didn't worry any more. It was only a step to the store and I had the money to get some new stock.

While I was putting my shoes on, the telephone started to ring down at the end of the hall. It rang for a long time and finally I heard the blonde's door bang and after a minute the ringing left off. I went on tying my shoes.

There was a knock on my door. When I opened it, the blonde stood there, wrapped tightly in her faded robe, her hair wet and stringy around her face.

"Your name Cross?" she said.

"Yeah."

"Telephone," she said, and went back into her room.

I made it to the phone after a while. Suddenly it seemed like a long trip to the end of that hall. When I picked up the dangling receiver it was like lifting a bucket of wet cement.

"Yeah," I said into the phone.

"Cross?" It was Foster's voice.

"Oh, hell!" I said. "Leave me alone."

"I wish I could." His voice was full of suppressed rage. "But it has come to my attention that you have a loose tongue."

I stood there, holding the receiver, trying to work up the energy to hang up on him.

"Let me remind you," he said, "that you can be put away for a long, long time. One more slip from you and I will see that this is arranged. Believe me, I can do it."

I stood there some more and he didn't say anything.

"Foster?" I said.

When he said, "What?" I made an obscene and impossible suggestion and hung up.

Back in my room I poured out the remaining shot from my bottle and drank it. I had to fight to keep it down. Still, it felt good afterward.

In the joint at the corner I had coffee and eggs and looked at the papers. One of them was the tabloid I had telephoned the day before. When I picked it up, I felt a sudden, lunging fear. But there was no banner headline. I got brave and turned to the inside.

On page 3 there was a one-column cut of a girl, eleven or twelve years old. The caption read: "Missing Girl Back Home?" Below it was a two-inch story about a mysterious phone call, possibly from a crank. The paper was checking up, but the caller had hung up before his identity or whereabouts could be learned. Efforts to contact Miss Jean Jordan had been futile. And that was all.

Well, I thought, maybe that was enough.

I stayed in the joint till after dark, drank some more coffee, walked up the street to the liquor store and bought a bottle, then headed back to the hotel.

I was feeling pretty good, but I was still weak and halfway up the stairs I had to stop and rest, clinging to the banister, clutching my bottle to my chest. The stairs and the hall at the top were dark, dingy and deserted. I guessed all the other tenants were out. I wondered where the blonde was and how she was doing. I wondered whether she would be worth cultivating.

I found my way to my room. The door was closed but I had left it unlocked. I pushed it open, walked in and stopped suddenly. Something had changed. It was dark, but even in the dark you can see shadows. And I was seeing shadows that had not been there the night before.

I was scared all right, but not petrified. I reached back with my left hand and found the light switch beside the door, snapped it up. Light flooded the room and the strange shadows turned into men. Two of them. One sat on the edge of the bed, the other in the chair at the foot of it. The one on the bed looked familiar but I couldn't place him. The one on the chair was my good friend, Roger "Scarface" Poole.

I stood there staring at them. The one on the bed got up, came to me, took the bottle out of my hand and set it on the dresser. He slid behind me, closed the door and leaned against it. He was short and stocky. He looked as if he were the same width from shoulders to floor.

Poole lit a cigarette. He got up from the chair and held the pack toward me.

"I don't smoke," I said.

He put the pack away. He took a long drag on the cigarette and blew the smoke out slowly.

"This will hurt you more than me," he said. "You made a stupid kind of mistake."

"We all make mistakes," I said.

He shrugged. I saw his eyes shift toward the thick guy behind me. But my reactions were sluggish and even if I had been able to move, there wasn't really anywhere to go. It was a small room.

I struggled briefly when I felt the stubby one's hands hard on my arms behind, dragging them back, twisting them to hold me. But I didn't have a chance. I couldn't have put up a good fight against a cocker spaniel pup.

At the last moment, I opened my mouth to yell, thinking there might be somebody home somewhere, but I never got the yell out. I saw the white scar beside Poole's nose and the way his cigarette jumped slightly in his mouth as his shoulders hunched. But I never saw what hit me—hit me so hard it felt like a sixteen-pound shot swung at the end of a long chain. There was horrible, crunching pain in my nose and blood in my mouth and I couldn't see any more. I tried to yell then, but choked on it and then the shot was hitting me in the chest and belly. I couldn't breathe. I had the feeling of panic you get when you can't catch a breath and back of the pain in my face was a swelling as if my head were being blown full of air. I must have tried to struggle again because there was a wrenching at my arms. But that went away and gradually the other pain faded. The slugging went on—I don't know how long—but all I could feel was the shock of it hitting me. I guess it went on till I was clear out, because I never felt myself hit the floor.

KISS ME HARD | 121

* * * *

I was still on the floor as life came back along with the pain. I was on the floor and I could breathe through my mouth, but every time I breathed it felt as if somebody were kicking me in the ribs.

I got my eyes open and blinked against the light, trying to see who was with me. It couldn't be Poole now because I knew he didn't wear perfume—dime-store perfume, the only kind I could have smelled with my broken, clogged-up nose. I saw a blurred shape but it hurt too much to look, so I closed my eyes again. A woman said, "Can you move?" And then, "What happened?"

I couldn't answer the first question because I didn't know and the answer to the second would be too long. I tried moving an arm and it moved all right, but when I tried to raise myself on one elbow my chest gave out and I flopped back onto the floor.

"You need a doctor," she said.

I figured out who she was—the blonde from the next room, being neighborly.

"Do you know a doctor?" she asked.

"Yeah," I said, the words rattling in my throat. "Brockman. Philip Brockman. He might come, if you tell him it's Chris Cross."

"Who?"

"Don't laugh. It's my name."

"O.K."

The smell of the perfume went away. I heard her heels going down the hall. I rolled over slowly, got my hands under me and pushed myself up painfully to my knees. I crawled to the bed and after a while managed to get up on it. It hurt too much to lie on my stomach so I rolled over again. The blonde came back. I saw that she was fully dressed, not wearing the pink bathrobe. She looked pretty good.

"He'll come," she said. "Shall I take off your shoes?"

"Are they still on?" I said.

She pulled the shoes off, straightened me on the bed and pulled a blanket over me. She went away again and when she came back she had a wet washcloth and some towels. The cool damp felt good on my face.

"I was coming in," she said, as she cleaned up my face. "Your door was open. What happened?"

"Couple of old friends dropped by," I said. "Let's have a drink."

She found my new bottle on the dresser and poured out a couple of shots. She sat in the chair beside the bed. We sat there drinking. The whisky felt good, but it hurt to move, even an arm or foot.

After a while there were footsteps in the hall and she went to the door and let Doc Brockman in. He was carrying a black bag. He stood by the door a minute, looking at me, then he said, "I don't know. I haven't made a call like this for ten years."

"What kind of doctor are you?" the blonde asked.

He smiled at her.

"A head doctor."

She shrugged.

"Well," she said, "I guess it's his head that hurts."

He came to the bed and pulled back the blanket.

"Where else does it hurt?" he said.

"Everywhere," I said.

He looked at the blonde.

"I'll have to get his clothes off," he said. "Want to help?"

"Why not?" she said. "I always wanted to be a nurse."

"What happened?" Doc asked as they went to work. "You get in a fight with a piano?"

"Let's put it that way," I said.

He didn't say any more then, but went ahead fixing me up. The blonde helped him. When they got through I was a solid mass of adhesive tape from my navel to my neck and there was a splint in my nose and tape over it, anchored on both sides to my cheeks.

Doc shook some pills out of a glass tube into a flat tin box.

"This is codeine," he said. "Help you sleep. How much have you had to drink in the last few days?"

"Hell of a lot," I said.

Doc got out a stethoscope and went over my chest with it. When he put it away he handed the box of pills to the blonde. To me he said, "You better switch from alcohol to dope," he said. "Don't try to mix them." To the blonde he said, "Let him have one of these every four hours. Only one."

"O.K.," she said.

"Got any money?" Doc asked me.

"Couple of dollars."

He sighed. He took out his wallet and pulled out some money, handed it to the blonde. She looked at him.

"I'm a lush, like him," she said.

He looked at the box of codeine in her hand.

"Are you on junk too?" he asked.

"No," she said.

He picked up his bag.

"All right," he said. "It's only money. I guess it's the only time a doctor ever paid the patient."

"I'll pay it back," I said.

"I know," Doc said. "With music. Eight dollars a bar?"

"You're on."

He went to the door.

"I'd keep this locked," he said. "You never know who might come in."

"Surely," I said. "Thanks, Doc."

He went out. I pointed to the bottle and the blonde shook her head.

"Uh-uh," she said. "Have a pill."

"I have to have something to take it with."

"Water," she said.

She went out. I started to get out of bed to get the bottle, but everything seemed to shift inside when I moved and I gave it up. The blonde came back with a glass of water and I took one of the pills.

"I'll go now," she said. "If you want anything, just pound on the wall."

"Thanks for helping," I said. "You can have the bottle."

"I figured on it," she said.

She went out, taking the bottle. She locked the door from the outside, then slid the key back under the door so I could get out if I had to. She was a good kid. I feel asleep thinking about her.

CHAPTER 15

She was faithful and good to me. She brought me two more codeine pills that night and in the morning she went down and got breakfast and brought it up to the room. We ate it together. I could get back and forth to the bathroom all right, but the rest of the time that first day I wasn't up to anything but sleeping. I woke up once the following night and couldn't get back to sleep. She brought me another pill and after that I could get along all right without them.

I dreamed a lot and a lot of it was about Connie. But the dreams weren't so much nightmares as before when I had been drunk. When I was awake I would remember the dreams and think about them and little by little as I thought about the situation, one particular idea kept coming back again and again. As the pain in my body dulled, my mind grew clearer and the thoughts got sharper and more sensible. Among the thoughts was the memory of some limited experience with tape recorders. You could do anything with tape. You could record a conversation, cut it up and put it back together almost any way you wanted to. And it would not be noticeable to the casual listener.

What would you do, I asked myself, if you had big money, like Jean Jordan had, and your long lost brother came back to claim half of it and you didn't want to share it? What if the long lost brother came back in a beat-up condition, half out of his mind with fear and frustration? How would you handle it—take care of him so there wouldn't be any publicity—and still hang onto all the money?

Naturally, I thought, you would have a lawyer, a real good, smart lawyer, and you could afford him all right. He would be sharp enough to see that the long lost brother was temporarily incompetent to handle his own half of the fortune and he might come right out and say this. So after you heard it from your own faithful attorney, you would maybe begin to wonder—why shouldn't this temporary condition become permanent?

You would have to make a deal with your attorney, cutting him in on more of your fortune than he had been getting before. But that would be better than splitting it fifty-fifty with your long lost brother. There wouldn't be much danger of blackmail, because once the attorney was in on it, you'd be even; you'd have as much on him as vice versa.

But what if the long lost brother wasn't quite so far gone as he seemed to be? What if all he needed was a little rest and a chance to get readjusted and then he would be all right again?

In that case, you would have to help him in reverse. You would have to make sure that he would go clear out of his mind and stay that way. If you did it thoroughly enough, you could maybe get him committed to an institution and let the state take care of him. That way, you wouldn't even have to pay his food bill.

I sat up on the bed and stared at the wall.

But how would you do that? How would you make sure?

I didn't know. I was a piano player, not a psychiatrist. But up to that point, I had a situation that seemed logical.

Late in the afternoon of the day that thought came through clearly, Doc Brockman came and took the splint out of my nose. It was a big relief. The blonde was there and she brought the bottle in and we all had a drink, Doc sitting in the chair at the foot of the bed. After a while the blonde went away and I said to Doc, "What happened to me was that a couple of bastards came in and beat me up."

"They did a good job," Doc said.

I let it sit there in his head for a while and then I said, "I keep thinking, they may come back."

"You could call the cops."

"No, Doc," I said. "Right now I couldn't."

He looked at me steadily across the bed.

"What did you have in mind?"

"I was wondering," I said, "whether you happen to have a gun."

There was a long pause, then he said, "I do happen to have a gun; two of them."

"Well, I wonder whether it would be a violation of medical ethics for you to lend me one of your guns, just temporarily, till I can move around and find another hideout."

The pause this time was very long.

"Chris," he said finally, "I worry about you. I do this because I have a weakness for music and you are, potentially, a great musician."

"Thank you," I said.

"I have a picture in my mind of you and a gun, both of you loaded, and somebody getting killed."

"I'd be afraid to shoot the damn thing except in self-defense," I said. "Maybe even then."

"You are already into me for the loan of a car, two professional calls and a dozen codeine tablets."

"I may be into you for more calls if those muscle men come back."

He frowned.

"Can't you tell me anything about it?" he said.

"Later," I said. "Not now."

He thought about it for a long time and then he got up and opened his bag. He dug around in it and came up with a small, pearl-handled revolver, maybe a .32. Big enough for what I might need. He laid it on the chair beside the bed.

"Just remember what happens," he said, "if somebody gets killed with a gun registered to me."

"I won't forget."

"Be sure," he said.

He took his bag and went out. I gave him plenty of time to get gone and then I got out of bed slowly and began to dress.

It took a long time. Pain and weakness blended to make me practically helpless for long periods. But when I had my clothes on and had moved around some, strength came back little by little. My nose started to bleed and I put a cold-water pack on it, and it stopped finally. When I got back to the room, the blonde was there with a sack full of food. I sat down on the edge of the bed.

"What are you doing up?" she said.

"Can't sleep forever," I said.

We ate the food. It helped. When we finished I stood up, poured out whisky for the two of us and we drank it. I straightened my clothes and walked around the room. I felt pretty good. I had put the gun in my coat pocket and when I lurched once against the dresser as a leg gave out, the pocket banged against the wood. The blonde got up slowly.

"You got any of that money left that the Doc gave you?" I asked.

"Some," she said.

"I'll split it with you."

"Where are you going?"

"I have to go out."

She looked at me and then she reached out and patted my coat pocket with her hand.

"What's that for?" she asked.

"Protection," I said. "How about the money?"

She studied me for a while, then went to her room. When she came back she had a handful of bills.

"There's twenty-eight dollars," she said, "and some change."

"I'll take fourteen," I said. "Keep the change."

"Thanks," she said.

I put the money in my pocket. She was watching me and when I looked at her face there was a look in it that I hadn't seen in her face before, a reaching-out look. It embarrassed me.

"You were good to me," I said. "Thank you."

She shrugged.

"You going to go rescue your rich little sweetheart?" she said.

"The honest-to-God truth is," I said, "I don't know. I have to try."

She turned away.

"I guess so," she said.

"I'll look you up—if I come back," I said.

She didn't look at me.

"I move around," she said.

"Thanks again."

"Don't mention it."

She kept her back to me as I went out of the room, left the hotel and went to the corner at Hollywood Boulevard to catch the Beverly Hills bus. On the bus I sat down in the last seat, close against the wall, so it would be hard for anybody in the street to see me.

At the Beverly Hills Hotel I got off the bus and found a cab. It took me to the front gate of the Jordan mansion, where I dismissed it. As I walked in the dark up the long, curving drive to the house, I felt stronger than I had for weeks. My knees were still weak, but inside I was steady and calm. The revolver dragged a little on my pocket.

There were lights inside the house, but the blinds were down and the front door was dark. I had to feel around to find the big knocker. When the Filipino opened the door and saw me, he started to close it again in my face. I put my shoulder against it and pushed him back into the room. I went in after him and kicked the door shut.

"I want to see Constance Jordan," I said.

He shook his head. His brown face was impassive.

"Cannot be disturbed," he said.

"Where is Jean Jordan?"

"Miss Jordan not home."

The door from the reception hall into the living room was open a few inches. I heard the faint clink of ice in a glass. I walked toward the door and the Filipino ran after me.

"Nobody home," he said.

In the living room, Jean Jordan was standing beside the coffee table with a long drink in her hand. She was alone in the room.

"I came to see Connie," I said.

She set the glass on the table.

"Connie isn't to be disturbed," she said.

She picked up the glass again and put some more liquor in it. She acted as if I had left the room. I crossed to where she stood and knocked the glass out of her hand. She swung on me and I caught her wrist and held it while we glared at each other.

"Lee," she said, "show the man out."

I glanced around and saw Lee, the Filipino, approaching uncertainly. I pulled the blonde's wrist down and swung her into him. They both went to the floor and rolled over. I ran to the staircase with the wrought-iron railing and started up, two steps at a time. I was winded at the top, but I went on down the hall, toward the end room where Connie had found the toys and the monkey puppet. A threat of light showed under the locked door.

Jean Jordan was coming down the hall.

"Open it," I said.

She opened her mouth to refuse, then closed it and shrugged her shoulders.

"All right," she said. "See for yourself."

She brought out a key, unlocked the door and stepped back. I brushed past her into the room, the child's bedroom we had seen that night a week before, with the Hollywood bed in the corner by the windows.

Connie was on the bed, lying on her back. She was wearing a harness-like contraption with straps and I couldn't see her arms or hands.

I walked to the bed slowly. Jean Jordan followed me.

"Connie—" I said.

She glanced at me but her eyes were flat and lifeless.

"Connie, honey," I said, "look at me."

I knelt beside the bed. She looked up at me then and her eyes looked alive and aware. After a moment they slid away toward Jean and the spark went out again.

I got up and turned to Jean.

"What's she wearing?" I asked.

"A strait jacket," she said. "Are you satisfied now?"

"Get out of the room," I said.

"I won't leave her alone with you—"

"Get out!"

I moved toward her and she backed away. She was holding the door key in her hand and I grabbed it and put it in my pocket. When she got outside, I closed the door in her face and went back to the bed.

"Connie, baby," I said, "don't you remember me?"

After a few seconds, the life came back to her eyes.

"Chris," she said.

She struggled under the strait jacket and I worked feverishly, unbuckling the straps to free her. When I got it off, I found she had nothing on under it.

"I couldn't say it when Jeanie was here," she said. "I promised. She made me promise."

"Promise what?"

"To forget you. She said you had gone away and would never come back."

"They told you that in Foster's office?"

"No. They told me I was sick. They said if I would go home with Jean, they would take care of me and then you would come when I was all right."

Her face was thin and pale and the dark circles under her eyes were larger than before. There were faint bruises here and there, near her eyes and one ugly bruise on her neck.

She was still clinging to me and I loosened her arm, let her down on the bed and started opening drawers in the chiffonier. I found a pair of panties that might fit her, and the white dress she'd bought in Westbrook. There were shoes and ankle socks near the bed. I began to dress her and she lay still, now and then helping me.

"What are we going to do?" she asked.

"We're going away."

"We can't," she said. "They'll stop us. I tried to get away, but they caught me. It hurts when they catch you."

I fastened her shoes and lifted her to the edge of the bed.

"Connie," I said, "I love you. I'm going to take care of you. But we have to go somewhere else."

She shook her head dully.

"There's no place to go. They won't let us."

"We're not asking them," I said.

"It doesn't matter. I tried to get away. Jean said I had to stay here, to get well. But I kept feeling worse. Sometimes I felt like I used to when I was a little girl."

"But I'm here now," I said. "I'm going to help you."

I felt frantic inside. Jean Jordan wouldn't stand around idle while I talked to Connie. She would be busy. She could have a whole cordon of cops around the house in a short time; or worse, she could have Poole and his sidekick, Shorty.

"Can you walk, honey?" I asked.

"Yes," she said.

I led her across the room and opened the door. There was nobody in the hall to get in our way. Downstairs I saw little Lee with his back against the door to the reception room. Jean Jordan was at a telephone on the opposite side of the room. I took the gun out of my pocket as we started down the steps. It felt good in my hand.

Jean Jordan saw us and hung up the phone.

"Lee—" she said.

I waved the gun.

"We're leaving," I said. "Get away from the door."

I aimed the gun at him and he looked at Jean. There was the sound of a car engine outside on the drive.

"You won't get far," Jean said.

"I don't have to get far," I said. "Lee, get away from that door."

He moved away toward Jean. The blonde took a couple of steps toward us, then stopped. I opened the door and we went into the reception hall. The front door opened and a guy came in. It was Foster. He blinked at us rapidly with those brows.

"What's going on here?" he said.

"Get away from the door," I said.

"You're mad, Cross," he said. "You can't pull a—"

"See the gun?" I said. "You think I won't use it?"

He looked at the gun and stepped out of the way. I led Connie through the door and kicked it shut behind us. There was a Cadillac parked in front of the house. I guessed it was Foster's. We went to the car and I opened the door and got Connie onto the front seat. I crawled in beside her and found the keys were in the slot. Foster's voice followed us, shouting, as I started it, got the lights on and drove the big car down the drive toward the street. Connie sat stiff and straight beside me.

CHAPTER 16

I parked the Cadillac across from the Beverly Hills Hotel, leaving the keys in it. Maybe somebody would steal it. They'd have a hell of a time convincing the cops I had taken it the first time.

I led Connie by the hand to a cab parked in front of the hotel and told the driver to take us to Doc Brockman's address. After we got started I reached across the seat for Connie's hand. She let me take it for a minute, then pulled away and shrank into the corner, watching me. It made me cold inside.

There were no lights in Doc's house and I stood at the door, holding Connie with one hand, punching the bell with the other.

He's got to be home, I thought. He has got to be here!

After an endless time a light went on somewhere inside and finally the door opened and Doc stood there in a dressing gown, looking out at us. His hair was rumpled.

"Sorry to get you up," I mumbled.

He looked past me at Connie, then opened the door wider and I led Connie inside.

"You remember Doctor Brockman, honey," I said.

She looked at him, and then she shrank back against me.

"Hello, Connie," Doc said. "Won't you come in and sit down?"

We followed him to a study off the living room. There was a desk in it and a studio couch. Doc motioned us to the couch and switched on a lamp. Connie sat stiffly beside me. Doc sat down in a chair near the desk and leaned forward, watching her. After a while he said, "Maybe Chris would get us a glass of water."

I got up from the couch. As I started out of the room, Doc said, "He'll have to let it run a long time to get it nice and cold."

I went to the kitchen and turned on the cold water. I leaned there against the shelf, my fingers tight on its edge, hearing the water run, fighting the waves of fear that kept rising, fear that I'd got there too late, that Connie was really sick now, beyond help.

Pretty soon I opened a cupboard, found a glass and got a drink of water for myself. It kept sticking in my throat. I had just finished it when a bell sounded faintly over my head. I started, thinking it was the doorbell.

Then it came again, quietly, three rings in rapid succession. I guessed it was Doc telling me to come back. I filled a couple of glasses with water and carried them into the study.

Connie lay on the studio couch with a blanket over her. The Doc's bag was open on his desk. He took one of the glasses and nodded toward the couch. We went over there.

"Connie," he said, "Chris brought you a drink of water." She looked up at me. "I'd like you to take this little pill now. You'll feel a lot better."

I sat on the edge of the couch, got an arm under her shoulders and helped her up. The Doc handed me a dark capsule. After a moment, Connie opened her mouth, the Doc nodded at me and I put the capsule on her tongue. I held the glass to her lips and she drank some of the water. I let her down gently and she lay still with her eyes on the ceiling.

Doc tapped my shoulder with a finger and motioned me toward the kitchen. In there he got down a bottle of whisky and a glass and offered it to me. I shook my head.

"How is she?" I said.

He seemed to think it over.

"I don't really know," he said. "Without the history, I can't tell."

"I can give you the history."

"I'm sure you can," he said, "but maybe this isn't the time for it."

He walked across the kitchen, paused, turned and started back. As he passed me on the return trip, he tapped the back of his hand against my right coat pocket.

"Did you have to use it?" he asked.

"No," I said.

I took the gun out of my pocket and handed it to him. I hated to let go of it. I kept thinking about how easy it would be for Poole to find us, if he got right on the ball. Once they found the Cadillac... But the Doc was talking to me, jerking me out of the thought.

"Try to see me, Chris," he said, "not as a friend, but as a doctor. A few nights ago you were here with this girl and I mentioned she looked ill. Naturally, later, when she looked ill to you too, you brought her back to me."

"All right," I said.

"She's ill. No question about it. I think she will get well. But in order to get well, she needs rest and care and seclusion. Would you say she needs seclusion?"

"Brother," I said.

"Right now she's in a kind of crisis. We have to ease her through that. Later, we can go into the history and, if necessary, develop some therapy that will speed her recovery. Does that sound all right to you?"

"You're the doctor," I said.

"Very well," he said. "Now I have three questions. They're important. I ask them as a doctor to whom you brought the girl in the night."

"O.K."

"Number One: has the girl committed any crime?"

"No."

"Good. Number Two: have you committed any crime—in connection with this girl?"

I looked at him. He looked back at me, his eyes large and unblinking.

"Would you treat the girl," I said, "even if I had committed some crime—in connection with her?"

He nodded.

"I would," he said.

"Is it a crime to go outside the law to save an innocent life?" I asked.

He thought that one over.

"Morally—no," he said. "And a strong moral case is a strong legal case."

"Then I'm in the clear," I said.

He straightened in the shoulders as if shrugging off a heavy weight.

"The third question is the most important of all," he said. "What do you feel for this girl? What does she mean to you?"

I met his eyes head on in the bright kitchen light.

"I tell you the truth, Doc—if she had to go there, I would take her to Shangri-La—personally—in my own arms."

He smiled a little, took my arm and led me into the living room. There was a telephone on a stand and he dialed a number. When someone answered, he spoke into the phone slowly and carefully.

"This is Philip, Mary. Could you go out to the desert for a few days, with a patient and a male attendant?... I know, but it's complete except for landscaping and everything is in order... Fine... Thanks, Mary. A gentleman will pick you up in my car in half an hour."

He put the phone down and turned to me.

"Two other doctors and I have this private hospital near Palm Springs," he said. "It's not open officially, but everything in it is ready to function. You may take Connie there. The girl I just talked to is a registered nurse named Mary Rice. Mary will go along and stay. I'll write instructions for her. I'll get down myself soon, possibly tomorrow night. Connie will get rest there, and sunshine and seclusion. Her name will appear as a registered patient in the hospital. It won't have to appear anywhere else."

"Who's this 'male attendant' you mentioned?" I asked.

"That is you. You have just been hired."

"I can use the work," I said.

"There'll be plenty. Mary can show you. Do you have any money?"

"A few dollars."

"That's what I thought."

He unlocked a drawer in the telephone stand and brought out some money.

"Wages in advance for one month," he said. "You'll have to stop and get food. Mary can do the shopping."

I put the money in my pocket. Doc stood up, rubbing the back of his neck with his hand.

"It all costs money, Chris," he said.

"I know. I don't have any. But Connie has. You might have to sue her sister to get it."

"I'll take a chance," he said. Then he laughed softly. "A chance the man takes! On a broken-down piano player and a girl from nowhere."

"All right," I said, "I may be broken down. But I'll put myself back together."

"I hope so," he said. "I still like to hear a good piano well played."

"Listen, Doc," I said, "a few days ago I played a good piano—good music. I found out I can still do it. I can get it back. Also I can stop drinking."

He was staring at me.

"When I was a little kid, when the other kids were out playing ball, raising hell—me, I was practicing on the piano. All right. I learned real good how to play the piano. And that's all anybody ever cared about. Nobody cared about me—as a guy!"

I stopped. There was a period of silence and then Doc said quietly, "Go on, Chris."

I jerked my head toward the study.

"That kid in there—she cares! About me. About music—maybe. But mostly about me, as a guy. And I care about here—as a girl. What more do I need?"

There was some more silence. Then Doc smiled and slapped my shoulder.

"O.K.," he said. "You've just had your first session of analysis. No charge."

He went into the study. After a while I followed him. The Doc was folding some papers into an envelope. He handed it to me. "Instructions to Mary," he said. "She knows where to call me."

I put the envelope in my pocket and Doc went out to get his car. I heard him backing it alongside the house. He stopped at a side door that opened into the study.

"I think she'll sleep till you get there," he said. "It's important that she not be alone when she wakes up. Either you or Mary will have to stay with her."

I picked Connie up and carried her to the car. We put her in the back seat and Doc wrapped the blanket around her. He told me where to find Mary.

"One more thing, Chris," he said. "You can trust Mary."

We shook hands. I couldn't think of anything to say.

* * * *

A bright moon lighted the road back toward the mountains and the low, rambling buildings of the hospital at their base. It was the hot season in the desert and even the night air was warm against my face. Mary directed me to a parking area at the rear of the buildings and asked me to wait while she turned on some lights and got the air conditioner going. She disappeared toward the front of the central building.

Lights appeared inside and then a big rear door swung open and Mary came out wheeling a bright chrome stretcher. I got out of the car to help her.

"Might as well do it the easy way," she said. "She's less likely to be disturbed."

We got Connie onto the stretcher and I followed Mary inside, carrying the big box of groceries we'd got at an East Side market.

There was a central rotunda with doors opening on two corridors. At the far end of each corridor was a set of French doors. The lights in the corridors were dim and warm. The stretcher made no sound on the linoleum floor.

"The kitchen is down there," Mary said, pointing to the corridor on my left. "If you'll take care of the groceries, I'll put Connie to bed. Room 19."

She went into the other corridor, wheeling the stretcher.

The rotunda had modern furniture around the walls. There was a receiving office near the front door, which was all glass, and farther along the wall a door with a frosted panel with three names on it. One of the names was Philip Brockman.

At the end of the corridor I found the kitchen, a large room with gleaming steel and porcelain fixtures and cupboards filled with dishes, pots and pans. I unpacked the box and stowed the food away. By the time I got back to Room 19, Mary was coming out into the corridor. She had left the door open and the room was dark behind her. I told her what I'd done with the food.

"Good," she said. "I'll get into something comfortable and sit with Connie. You'd better get some sleep."

"I can't sleep now," I said. "I'll sit with her."

She looked back into the room, and then at me thoughtfully. The palms of my hands were sweating and I rubbed them on my pants legs slowly.

"She means a lot to me," I said. "You know how it is?"

Mary smiled a little. For the first time I noticed that she was beautiful. She had red hair and clear, white skin. Her lips were full and curving and her figure was like a model's, small waist, square shoulders and the proper development between.

"All right, Chris," she said. "You sit with her. I'll sleep till six o'clock. If she wakes, don't speak to her unless she calls for something. If she seems frightened, try to comfort her, but if you can't, please call me. There's a bell beside the bed."

"Thanks, Mary," I said.

She started away down the corridor. After a few steps she turned back to look at me.

"Yes," she said, "I know how it is. What do you think would get me up in the middle of the night to come to the desert—in the summertime?"

She went on then and turned into a room at the far end of the corridor. I watched her out of sight, then walked into Connie's room and sat down in the easy chair near the bed.

She knows how it is, I thought. She's in love too. With Brockman. I guess she would do for him the same things I've tried to do for Connie—and maybe more than that.

I looked at Connie. Moonlight came through the window, lighting her face.

Sleep, baby, I thought. You're among friends now. For a while now.

CHAPTER 17

Connie woke several times, but she didn't stay awake long and she never cried out. I got up each time to see that she was covered. The last time she woke it was beginning to grow light and I couldn't get back to sleep myself. I sat and watched the sun rise over the desert till Mary came and sent me out to take a dip in the pool.

They had a big swimming pool, full of green water. There was a wide patio around it with cabanas and at one end a sundeck with three or four patio lounges. The sun was plenty hot now, though it was early, and I could feel it hit me as I stripped down by the edge of the pool. I couldn't dive in with that nose I had, so I lowered myself into it and swam leisurely to one end, fighting the tape around my chest. I hung onto the overflow ledge for a while, catching my breath, before climbing out.

My skin was pale and sick-looking. I had what we used to call a "barroom tan." A few weeks out here in the sun, with a swim every day, no liquor and plenty of good food, would begin to put me in shape.

Then I thought, how in hell do I know that? I've never been in good shape. I don't know what it would be like.

* * * *

We had breakfast in Connie's room and afterward I took the trays to the kitchen and washed the dishes. When I got back to the room afterward, it was empty. I stood in the corridor for a couple of minutes and Mary appeared at the far end.

"We're out on the sundeck," she said.

I walked that way and Mary stopped me at the door.

"I don't know—" she said. "We had to improvise a sunsuit for her. It's brief."

Connie's voice came from outside.

"Chris?"

Mary shrugged.

"Go ahead," she said. "Health comes first."

Connie was lying on a chaise longue on the ivy-roofed sundeck. The sunsuit was a wisp of cloth between her legs, gathered low in front, with a narrow band around her hips. There was another narrow band that partially covered her breasts.

"You take off your clothes, too, Chris," Connie said.

Mary shrugged again.

"It's up to you," she said. "I have to drive into town. I'll get some clothes for Connie. We've talked it all over."

She went away.

"Aren't you going to take off your clothes?" Connie said.

"Sure, honey."

I took them off and stretched out on a chaise beside her. Pretty soon I heard the Doc's car start and the scrape of its tires on the gravel parking. A minute later it appeared on the road leading to the highway. Then it disappeared again and Connie and I were alone.

"It looks nice up there," Connie said.

I looked in the direction she was pointing. From the open end of the sundeck we could see part of the mountain behind the hospital and the range to the south. A few hundred yards to the south, farther back from the highway, was a small arroyo cut between the gray-brown mountains. Trees grew in it, well down onto the desert floor.

"Maybe someday," Connie said, "we could go up there and have a picnic."

"We'll go," I said. "When you feel well and strong."

"Will we, Chris? Will we do it?"

I took her hand, squeezed it gently.

"We'll do whatever you want to do."

She raised herself on one elbow and the strip of cloth across her breasts fell away. I reached over to replace it but I couldn't make it stay. Connie grinned at me slyly.

"Chris," she said, "remember the hotel?"

"I remember," I said.

"Could we do that again?"

"Now?" I said. "What about Mary?"

Her face clouded. I was sorry I'd said it.

"Mary won't care," she said.

I began to get scared. I didn't know what it would do to her. I didn't know whether she should do that now or not. But also, I didn't know what it would do to her if I refused.

I looked into her eyes. They were bright and clear. She wasn't mixed up in her head now. Or was she? How could I know? I wasn't a doctor.

"Don't you love me anymore, Chris?"

I sat up and put my arm around her shoulders, holding her close. She hid her face against my chest.

"I love you every way there is," I said. "I'll never leave you. We'll do whatever you want to do."

She snuggled closer against me, then pulled herself onto my lap, her arms tight around my neck. She put her mouth against my ear.

"Let's go in the room, Chris."

I picked her up and carried her inside and down the corridor to the room. I put her on the bed but when I leaned over her, she stiffened and pushed back, her little hands hard against my chest.

"Will you hurt me, Chris?"

"No, Connie. I won't hurt you. We don't have to do it now."

She stared up at me and little by little her body relaxed. She closed her eyes.

"I'm sleepy," she said.

I covered her with the sheet and a blanket and started out of the room. I pulled the door open, stepped into the corridor and ran into Mary. She took one startled look at me, then went on past.

"Excuse me," she said. "I'll be in my room—if you care to dress."

Her voice was cold.

I found her a few minutes later in the kitchen.

"I guess I'd better tell you what the score is," I said.

She wouldn't look at me.

"I guess you better tell me something," she said. "I'm not used to running a hospital all by myself."

"You're doing all right," I said.

She was fixing a light lunch and we sat down at a table in the kitchen to eat it. As we ate I told her the whole story, from the time I'd picked Connie up beside the railroad tracks. It took quite a while. I got to the point where Connie had asked me if we could do it again, as we had in the hotel. I told her about that, too, frankly and fully. I told her how Connie had pushed me away finally. When I finished, she got up and made a couple of turns around the room.

"It's unbelievable," she said. "But you're a friend of Phil's and I believe you."

"Thanks," I said.

She paced some more. I could see there was something on her mind, but I couldn't guess what it was. We did the dishes together and finally she got around to telling me.

"I called Phil when I was in town," she said. "He had a visit this morning—from an attorney named Foster."

I cleared my throat lightly.

"How did Doc take it?" I asked.

She looked at me in a new way; still gentle, still warm, but something else too—something that had to do with respect.

"I'm glad you asked that," she said. "You must know what a long limb he went out on for you."

"Yes," I said.

"He would have done it anyway, naturally," she said. "A sick girl came to him and he had to take care of her. Any doctor would do the same.

"But he told me, Chris, that if the girl is incompetent, even temporarily, her nearest of kin are responsible for her and can determine what to do with her until the law makes some other decision. Regardless of her age."

"So they want her back. What if Doc says she's too ill to be moved?"

"That would work for a while, but they'd have a right to call another doctor for consultation. Phil couldn't keep him out."

"I could take her over to Arizona and marry her. Who's the nearest of kin then?"

She shook her head slowly.

"She's too sick, Chris. Here in the hospital she feels secure. She remembers most things and she knows and loves you. But a little while ago, she wouldn't let you make love to her.

"She's on the borderline, Chris. If you were suddenly to put her in a car and take her away somewhere, she might really crack up. The way it is now, I'm sure she can get well."

"She'll crack up for good if they get her back," I said.

I walked around in a small circle and stopped in front of Mary's chair.

"How can they do it?" I asked. "How can they just come and take her away?"

"They'll have a scrap of paper ordering her release. They might have an officer with them."

"What if you refuse to release her?"

"They could take her by force, if necessary, and still be legal."

I thought about it. I thought about lying with Connie on the sundeck. I thought about the mountains.

"What if she wasn't here when they came?" I said.

Her eyes widened.

"Where would she be? I told you we couldn't move—" I told her about the arroyo and the grove of trees, about Connie wanting to go on a picnic. Mary got up and started pacing again.

"If you would take Connie up there," I said, "I could stay here. If they come here for her, I'll get rid of them. I don't think you'd have to stay long."

She gave me a long look.

"How would you get rid of them, Chris?"

"I'll think of something."

"But we don't even know for sure they're coming."

"They'll come. Those people move fast."

I rubbed the tip of my finger lightly over the tape across by nose. Mary ground out a cigarette in a tray beside the sink.

"All right," she said. "We'll try it. But remember, Chris, if anything should happen to you, there wouldn't be much point in Connie's getting well."

"O.K.," I said. "You'd better get ready for a therapeutic picnic. I'll hide Doc's car."

* * * *

I found a place to hide the car behind an abandoned shack a quarter of a mile from the hospital. Checking the glove compartment on a hunch, I had found a .38 pistol in a holster. I carried it back with me, the holster strapped to my belt. Mary was in the kitchen, packing a lunch basket.

"Connie's excited about the picnic," she said, "but she wants you to go along."

"What did you tell her?"

"I told her you had some work to do, that you'd come later and eat with us."

"I will," I said. "So help me."

She picked up the basket, and put a hand on my shoulder.

"Good luck, Chris," she said. "Take care of yourself."

"Sure," I said.

She went out with the basket and I stood in the kitchen waiting, giving them time to get on their way. She was a good kid. She couldn't have missed seeing the gun, but she hadn't mentioned it.

After a while I walked into the corridor, past Connie's empty room and down to the end, to the sundeck. I saw them walking, close to the mountain, Mary in her white uniform, Connie in a white dress that looked new. I stood watching till they had disappeared among the trees. Then I went back inside.

CHAPTER 18

The hospital was the same inside, but now I knew I was alone in it and it felt strange. My footsteps seemed to echo in the corridors. I had the feeling I was being followed.

In the rotunda I went to the door of the office with the doctors' names on it, opened it and looked inside. There were filing cabinets on one wall, a big safe on the opposite wall with the doors open, and in the middle of the room, a secretary's desk with a typewriter stand beside it. I took the gun out of the holster and laid it on the stand.

I began idly to look through the drawers of the desk. In the bottom right drawer was a tape recorder. I had always wanted one. Out of curiosity I plugged it in and began fooling around with it. There was a spool of tape already in recording position. I started it revolving and picked up the microphone.

Then I couldn't think of anything to say. I shut off the motor, but left the power on and laid the microphone on the desk. I looked around some more.

Beside the safe in the wall nearer the front of the building was a door with a transom, open now. The door led into the receiving office near the front entrance. It was an open room with a long counter, waist high. On top of a small desk was a printed card. It was an admittance form for the hospital. It had Connie's name on it, her age and the date she had entered the hospital. The initials M.R. were written in one corner.

I opened a drawer in the desk and dropped the card into it. I heard a far-off rumble and glanced through the window of the receiving office. A car was approaching from the direction of the highway, winding up the road toward the hospital. It looked as if it might be Foster's Cadillac. I went into the rotunda and looked out the glass door to get a better look at it. It kept coming and I saw it was the Cadillac all right.

I backed across the rotunda and came up against the door of the main office. The door swung open and I backed into the room. I glanced out once more and the big car was turning into the small parking area in front of the building. I closed the door to the receiving office and threw a snap lock. There was a lock on the door of the main office too and I threw that one, locking myself in.

Beside the door was a glass panel, maybe five feet high. I looked at it and noticed I was looking into the rotunda. I stepped back quickly before I saw that the glass was thick and rough and not like window glass. It was one of those one-way windows. I could see out, but nobody could see in.

I heard brakes and tires scraping outside. Doors slammed. I backed away from the panel and leaned against the desk. When I rubbed my hands together they were damp. I rubbed them dry against my pants legs. I picked up the gun a couple of times, weighed it first in one hand, then the other, and finally put it down again on the typewriter stand. Outside there were faint voices and I knew they were coming in.

It was a sharp angle toward the front door and I couldn't see them enter through the panel. But I could hear their feet shuffling on the floor and it sounded like quite a crowd.

Suddenly a bell rang, practically in my ear. I jumped and looked around and it rang again. I figured out that it must be a bell on the receiving office counter. It rang once more for a long time, then stopped and a voice said. "There must be somebody around. The door—" It was Foster's voice. Then came Jean Jordan's, thin and impatient.

"Well, ring it some more. We don't have all day."

The bell shrilled around me till I put my hands over my ears to shut out the sound. As it stopped finally, a shadow passed the glass panel beside the door and I made out the figures of two men, strolling toward the corridor. One of them, tall and broad-shouldered, was Roger Poole. The other, bulky, wide and squat, must be his ever-loving partner, Shorty.

They stopped walking while I could still see them and I knew they were talking together, but I couldn't hear the words. Foster and Jean were mumbling at each other, too, and I couldn't understand them either. Then Jean's voice rose sharply as she took over.

"The three of you," she said, "look through the place. If you don't find anyone, we'll call the Palm Springs police. I'll wait here."

There was the sound of tramping feet, spreading and fading as the men went into the corridors. Jean Jordan came into view through the panel. She sat down in a chair against the opposite wall of the rotunda and lit a cigarette.

On one end of the desk was a small switchboard. I lifted one of the phones on the desk and listened. There was a dial tone. As noiselessly as I could, I dialed Operator. A girl's lazy voice inquired insinuatingly, "Yes, please?"

My own voice was a harsh whisper. I hoped it sounded sinister—or just plain scared. "Give me the police."

Out in the rotunda Jean suddenly got up and started toward me. The room wasn't sound proof, and I couldn't afford to do any more talking. I'd have to count on the operator. If she was any good at all... Gently I put the phone down on the desk, leaving the line open. It sputtered for a moment, then was quiet. The operator had probably decided it was a crank call and closed the connection.

Beyond the one-way window Jean hesitated, moving the cigarette in and out of her mouth in jerky, nervous movements.

Go ahead, lady, I thought. Get good and nervous. Maybe you can get to be a candidate for a strait jacket yourself.

I looked back at my phone. Maybe I was taking a big chance—with Connie's sanity and my own neck—calling in the law. But I could count on Brockman's standing behind me. That is, if they ever came.

Footsteps approached from one of the corridors and Jean turned sharply, dropped her cigarette and stepped on it.

"Well?" she said.

"Nothing back there," Foster said. "A kitchen. It's been used."

More footsteps and Poole and Shorty walked past the glass panel. Poole was carrying something.

"There's a suitcase and some nurse's uniforms in the last room," he said. "I found these hanging on the line."

Jean looked over the laundry.

"They're hers all right," she said. "There's a telephone on that counter. Call the police."

"Just a minute," Foster said. "Are you sure you want to—?"

"I'm sure," she said. "What are you afraid of? You said you had an airtight case."

I straightened slowly. I noticed the microphone on top of the desk. I leaned over the open drawer and started the tape running through the mechanism. It made a slight rustling sound, but nothing that could be heard outside.

"Well?" Jean Jordan said harshly. "Do you have a case or don't you?"

"Certainly I have. But they may be building a case for themselves."

"What can they do?"

"They can make it pretty—embarrassing for us."

She said a nasty word and went to the counter. Her hand folded over the phone.

"Just a minute, Jean! Don't be premature. If the girl's things are here, she can't be far away. Why don't we try to relax—"

"And let that dirty lush bring her back in his own good time?"

I'll remember that, lady, I thought.

"Listen to me," Foster said. "We are not ready to bring in the police. You've forgotten Dr. Brockman."

"What about him?" Jean said contemptuously. But her hand came away from the phone.

"If he should say Connie is too ill to be moved, we'd have to take her by force. That would bring everything into the open."

"All right then!"

"It's not all right!" Foster had begun to shout. "We haven't got any doctors lined up on our side yet. You'll never keep that money till we do."

Poole broke in, calm and sure of himself.

"I think Foster is right," he said. "Better to wait and try persuasion."

I quit listening. I turned off the recorder and rewound the tape. It took only a few seconds. I stopped it, switched the machine to "play back" and turned the volume up.

Their voices crashed through the room. I knew they wouldn't have any trouble hearing it through the open transom. It drowned out whatever other sounds they were making and I let it run to the last bitter word. Then I switched it off abruptly.

There were a few seconds of dead silence. I yanked the two spools of tape off the machine and turned to the open safe against the wall. I heard Poole's voice saying, (...in that office..."

I threw the tape into the safe, slammed the door and twisted the tumbler. I ran back to the desk, picked up the gun and faced the door. A new voice came through. I guessed it to be Shorty's.

"I'll open it—locked or not."

There was a crash against the door. I aimed the gun at the middle of the door and squeezed the trigger. The blast drowned the splintering of the wood, but I saw the small, ragged hole where the bullet went through. Shorty gave a yelp of pain. There was a shuffling of feet.

"You stupid son of a bitch," Poole said. "Get out of the way."

There was a gun blast from outside and I ducked. But he wasn't shooting at me. He was trying to break the lock. It was a tough lock. He had to hit it twice more before the door was free of the latch. After a moment it swung slowly on the hinges till it stood wide open. There was nobody in sight through it. I guessed they were standing to one side, or maybe on both sides. I could see the color of Jean's dress through the panel.

Poole spoke.

"Come on out," he said.

"Come and get me," I said.

Jean cursed.

"I got you all on tape now," I said, "and it's going to take a bigger gun that Poole's to blast open that safe."

Foster's voice came.

"Now listen," he said, "I don't know what you think you've got. But that kind of evidence doesn't mean a thing in court—"

"I don't think you'll ever get to court," I said.

Jean Jordan started to crack up.

"Go get him, somebody!" she screamed.

Poole spoke quietly.

"There's a door leading in there behind that counter. I'll open it. You stay here. Jean, you'd better get out of the way."

"Just do something!" she said.

"Hold it!" I said loudly. I knew Poole could open the other door, and when he did, I was finished. I thought maybe it was time to start using the head instead of the muscle.

"Hold it," I said. "I'll come out. I don't know how many guns you've got. But I know I'm no good to you dead. You throw your guns on the floor where I can see them and I'll throw mine out too. Then I'll come out."

"The hell with it," Poole said.

"If you come after me with a gun," I said, "somebody's going to get hurt. Me, too, but somebody else first."

"Do what he told you," Jean said.

"But look—"

"Throw your gun down there!" she yelled.

There was a ringing thud and a small automatic slid across the floor, stopped in front of the open door.

"Shorty—" Jean said.

So his name really was "Shorty"!

Another gun plopped into sight on the floor. I took a deep breath and tossed my .38 out along with them. I walked slowly, stiff-legged, through the door and out into the rotunda. They waited, watching me silently. They were standing in pairs on each side of the door, Jean and Poole on my right and Foster and Shorty on my left. I walked between them to the middle of the rotunda, stopped, turned around and looked at them.

"I'll make a deal with you," I said.

"We don't have to deal," Jean said. "Where's Connie?"

"You have to deal if you want that tape out of the safe," I said.

There was a pause.

"Go ahead," Jean said. "What's your deal?"

I took another long breath.

"Right now Connie is sick. But she can get well. I've got the doctor who can make her well. If you'll pay the doctor and hospital bill, and if you'll leave both of us alone, we'll never try to cut in on the estate."

Jean looked at Foster. He shook his head.

"You'd never know," he said. "They could bring a suit for part of the estate at any time."

"Look," I said. "I have to trust you to leave us alone. You have to trust me to leave you alone."

"Deals aren't made on trust," Foster said. "We have to have security."

"Then so do I," I said.

"Naturally," Foster said.

Shorty was shuffling his feet impatiently. He was holding onto his left arm, where I must have winged him, shooting through the door.

"We going to stand around and talk?" he said. "I got to take care of my arm."

"The hospital is fully equipped," I said. "Help yourself."

He growled and started toward me. I backed away from him toward the wall, got my hand behind me on the arm of one of the chairs. I glanced at Jean Jordan. She stood there, watching Shorty. Nobody said anything to stop him.

I twisted my body to the left, gripped the chair arm with my right hand, swung back around and let go of it. It flew toward Poole. He threw up an arm, but it got him hard in the shoulder and he fell back against Jean. They both went over. Shorty jumped for me and I ducked to one side and grabbed the wrist of his wounded arm. He roared with the pain and I tried to swing him around. But there was blood on his wrist and my hand slipped off. I heard scrambling across the floor and knew Poole would be going for a gun. I ducked low, trying to get around Shorty before he found his balance. But he hit me with his fist on the back of my head and I fell on my face. The floor was cold and hard and I twisted my ankle as I went down and tried to roll out of the way. Then he kicked me in the ribs and my breath went away. He kicked me in the head and I felt myself going out, still gasping for breath.

There was the shock of cold water dashed into my face. I blinked, coming out of it. I was lying on my back on the floor. Shorty was leaning over me with an empty saucepan in his good hand. When he saw my eyes were open he threw the pan away and reached for me, grabbing the front of my coat. There was a dull, pounding ache in my head and nose. My ribs ached sharply and pain shot through my twisted ankle.

He yanked me to my knees, started to slap me with his other hand and yelled as the pain from his wound caught him. I let him pull me to my feet, found my balance and brought my right knee up hard into his crotch. He yelled again, let go of my coat and started to swing. I ducked under his fist and fell back against the wall.

Jean, Poole and Foster were standing in a line a few feet away, watching. Poole had a gun leveled on me. Shorty started to charge me again and Jean cried, "Wait!"

Shorty seemed glad to wait. He stood off four or five feet. I sucked in some air, leaning against the wall, supporting myself with one hand on the back of a chair. Jean walked toward me, stopped when she got even with Shorty.

"You'll only kill him that way," she said. "He knows where Connie is and I want to find out."

She came a half-step nearer and spoke to me.

"There's no need to go through all this," she said. "Tell us where Connie is and we'll leave you alone."

I stared at her through a kind of haze. Then I shook my head slowly and pointed to my ear, hoping she'd figure Shorty had kicked my hearing out of order. She came a step closer, not quite within reach, but closer.

"Where's Connie?" she said loudly.

I bent one ear toward her.

"What?" I said.

She brought up one hand in a gesture of exasperation. I caught her wrist, yanked her close to me. She started to struggle and I twisted her around, bringing the wrist up behind her back, putting pressure on it. She screamed. I caught the other wrist and dragged that back too. I locked them together, held them with one hand and pulled her back against me with one arm around her waist.

Poole had taken a couple of steps and he had the gun ready, but now he couldn't shoot me without shooting Jean too. I put more pressure on her twisted arms as she kicked at my shins with her heels. She quit kicking and hollered. I let up enough to make her listen.

"You seem to be the boss," I said. "Start giving orders. Tell them to get in the car."

She started to struggle again and I pushed her wrists up till she quit.

"Roger—!" she said.

He stood there with his gun and looked helpless. Shorty took a step toward us and I gave her a good treatment with the wrists. She screamed at him to stay back.

She was wearing a one-piece print dress with a zipper down the back. I tore at the zipper with my free hand, pulled it down to her locked wrists, reached up under them and pulled it the rest of the way down.

"You better start talking, sister Jean," I said. "You're going to be in an embarrassing position."

She kept quiet. Under the print dress she wore a nylon slip. I knew I couldn't tear it. And I knew she wouldn't stand still and let me take her clothes off if I let go of her arms.

I reached around in front of her, got a handful of skirt and slip and pulled them up over her head. She twisted frantically and I almost lost my grip on her wrists. Then I grabbed them with both hands and she settled down again. She was sobbing through the cloth over her face, shaking her head from side to side.

"Now, Cross," Foster said suddenly, "you're only making more trouble for yourself."

"Uh-huh," I said.

Shorty collapsed to the floor. There was quite a pool of blood under his shattered arm. Jean stood still and stiff against me, her chest heaving. I reached around and got hold of her brassiere, dragged down on it.

"Tell Poole to drop the gun," I said.

She mumbled something through the cloth.

"Speak up," I said.

This time we could hear the words.

"Drop the gun."

After a moment, Poole dropped the gun to the floor. Jean made a brief struggle. I reached in front of her again, got my fingers on the waistband of her panty girdle and pushed down on it.

"Tell them to put Shorty in the car," I said.

Her words came out clear this time.

"Do it," she said. "Do what he says!"

Foster and Poole leaned over and picked Shorty up. It wasn't easy. They lurched with him to the door and pushed through it. I couldn't see them after they went through the door. My hands were tired from holding Jean's wrists and I knew I couldn't hang on much longer.

Her next words were pleading, no longer dictatorial.

"Cover me up," she said. "Please."

"I can't hear you," I said. "He kicked me in the ear, remember?"

Her head dropped forward. I could feel her crying. Maybe it will do her some good, I thought.

The front door opened and Poole and Foster came back in. Poole started toward his gun and I said, "Leave it there. Go on back to the car. I'll bring her out."

They looked at each other uncertainly, then went back outside.

"Walk," I said to Jean.

We walked to the front door. It was awkward walking. I had to synchronize my steps with hers and she didn't walk very steadily. I peered out through the door at the Cadillac. The front door was open and Foster and Poole were sitting in the front seat. I couldn't see Shorty. He would be in the back.

Suddenly I felt weak. Something happened to my eyes and I was dizzy. Jean felt my grip loosen and tried to pull away and I forced myself to tighten my grip once more. She sobbed. I let go of her wrists and took hold of the wad of cloth around her shoulders, holding the slip and dress over her face. She moved her arms slowly, experimentally.

"The door is in front of you," I said. "Push it open."

She put her hands flat against the glass and pushed the door open.

"Walk straight ahead," I said.

She started, then stopped and stood there, limply, buckling at the knees. I put an arm around her waist, held her up and walked her to the car. She barked her shin climbing into the seat beside Poole. I looked across at them. My own knees were giving out on me and I had to talk in jerky phrases, with big breaths in between.

"Get going," I told Poole. "Don't come back. I've got three guns in there now. If you come back, I won't talk any more. I'll just start shooting."

I slammed the car door. Foster started the engine. I blinked my eyes and when I opened them, nothing had happened, the car hadn't moved. Suddenly the door opened and I had to step back to keep it from slamming me. Poole came charging out through it. I stepped back again, tripped and fell heavily on my side. It felt as if I had broken every rib in my body all over again.

Poole was on top of me, one of his knees digging into my left arm. I remember yelling at him, my throat burning with the effort, and the wild lunge I made to get him off of me. I remember feeling suddenly free and light, charging with head down, coming up against a smooth, hard surface that gave slightly. When I put my hand on it I found it was glass and I pushed hard against it. Behind me, Poole was cursing—close behind.

The glass door gave easily and I scrambled across the hard floor of the rotunda on all fours. My hand brushed against one of the guns and I grabbed it, swung on my heel and came down on my knees, facing the door. The gun was out in front of me and my hand was trembling.

I couldn't see very well, but well enough to know that Poole had come through the glass door, his mouth twisted. He was probably still cursing.

"Hold it!" I yelled.

I don't know whether I made any sound. There was a roaring in my ears and I couldn't be sure. He evidently didn't hear me, because he kept coming.

But both of us heard the high, whining scream of the police siren coming up from the valley. And that stopped Poole. He halted four feet from me, half-crouched, indecision breaking his face into small pieces.

Then he straightened slowly, his eyes glazing with panic, and began backing carefully, but faster now, toward the door, his hand out, feeling behind him. The door opened and he backed through it.

I lurched to my feet and went after him, still holding the gun. By the time I pushed through the door, Poole had flung himself into the already moving car.

The siren screamed again, closer this time.

Foster was crouched over the wheel, giving it everything he had. The car was already rocketing down the drive, spitting gravel. I aimed for the rear tires, and I guess I emptied my gun—but I didn't stop them.

Down near the highway the police car had just turned into the hospital road. Foster careened into the ditch and tore past, swinging onto the highway toward Los Angeles. The police car turned on a dime and raced after them.

I stood there swaying, staring at the empty road. Then I felt a strong hand on my arm, and I turned and saw Mary.

"They've gone," I said.

"Are you all right, Chris?" Mary said.

"I'm fine. How's Connie?"

"I had to bring her back. She got worried when you didn't come. Then I heard the shooting."

"I don't think they'll come back," I said. "But the police will."

She smiled firmly. "Let them. We'll be ready for them."

But I didn't want to think about that—yet. I started across the rotunda toward the corridor. Mary came along, holding my arm. The door of Connie's room was open and I walked down there and shook Mary's hand off my arm. She stayed in the corridor.

Connie was in bed with the covers up to her chin. She looked at me across the room.

"You missed the picnic," she said.

"I'm sorry," I said. "We'll have another one tomorrow."

I went down on my knees beside the bed. Connie's big brown eyes looked at me. She pushed the covers down and pulled my head onto her breast. I could feel her heart beating, brave and steady against my ear.

Made in United States
North Haven, CT
28 June 2024